## “Why are you in my bed?” Zach demanded

“It’s...my bed,” Hannah responded breathlessly.

“No...this is my bed.” He spoke slowly, thickly, as if he wasn’t quite awake. “Or at least it’s the one you gave me. I think. Am I in the wrong bed?”

No, he was in exactly the right bed. And now that her initial nervousness had worn off, Hannah was becoming aware of several things.

One, he smelled good. *Really* good.

Two, he felt good. *Really, really* good.

And oh yeah, as far as she could tell, he was nearly naked.

To test, she arched up, just a little, because wow, he felt incredible. She wasn’t really trying to take advantage of him, at least not until he woke all the way up—okay, maybe she was, just a little. She encountered...yep, more sleek skin and tough muscle.

No clothes.

At her movement, he’d gone completely still. And she could feel him become ever more...*awake!*

Dear Reader,

Ever fantasize? Okay, silly question. Well, in *Out of the Blue*, three best friends run a B and B and share a simple fantasy—to find a man. Any man, as long as he's smart, funny and *sexy*. In fact, they make a bet to see who can be the first to get one.

But my heroine, Hannah Novak, has a little problem. How is she to go about getting a man when she has absolutely *no* experience in the matter? But then Zach Thomas shows up, the town's sexiest bad boy, and she figures he'll know what to do. Only, he has no intention of letting Hannah seduce him to win a bet!

This story is my first for the *Wrong Bed* miniseries in Temptation. These books—with their sexy, sassy heroines and unique story lines—have always been some of my most favorite reads. And don't forget to watch for other *Wrong Bed* books in the coming months!

Happy reading,

Jill Shalvis

## Books by Jill Shalvis

HARLEQUIN TEMPTATION

742—WHO'S THE BOSS?
771—THE BACHELOR'S BED

HARLEQUIN DUETS

28A—NEW AND...IMPROVED?
42A—KISS ME, KATIE!
42B—HUG ME, HOLLY!

# OUT OF THE BLUE

## Jill Shalvis

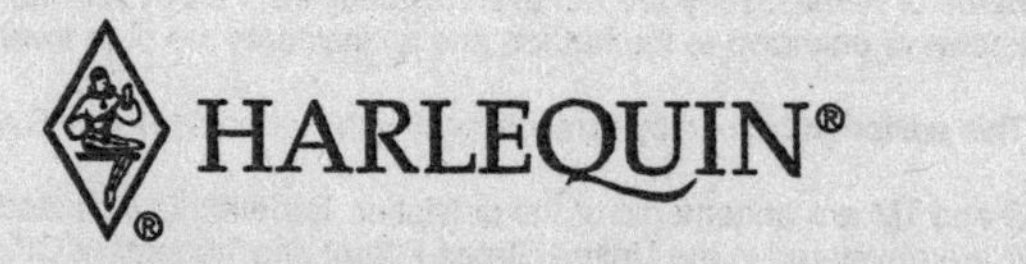


TORONTO • NEW YORK • LONDON
AMSTERDAM • PARIS • SYDNEY • HAMBURG
STOCKHOLM • ATHENS • TOKYO • MILAN • MADRID
PRAGUE • WARSAW • BUDAPEST • AUCKLAND

ISBN 0-373-25904-2

OUT OF THE BLUE



This edition published by arrangement with Harlequin Books S.A.



Visit us at www.eHarlequin.com

**Printed in U.S.A.**

# Prologue

ZACHARY THOMAS PLANNED to spend the entire next week in a prone position. Either on the sand with the warm sun over his face, in a hammock with the warm breeze brushing his limbs, or in a bed with a warm body beside him, it didn't matter.

Better yet, give him all of the above.

But he had to get there first, to Avila, before the exhaustion claimed him.

Ten years ago he'd left that town as the wild rebel. Today he was going home, still a rebel at heart, but now he was a cop as well.

He'd never thought it would happen, but after so long, he was really going back.

Home.

More figuratively than literally, since his childhood house no longer belonged in the family. It'd been sold long ago, his elderly parents having retired to Arizona. But in his mind, the popular beach town of Avila would always be the place to come home to. The place of sun and surf, fun and laughter.

God, he was exhausted, his body aching, and in the tight confines of his Jeep he stretched his travel-weary limbs the best he could. Every inch of him protested the four-hour drive north.

No doubt, working undercover all year, tracking a drug ring in the armpits of Los Angeles, had been tough on his body.

So had getting shot.

But thankfully he was healing, more and more every day, and the case was over. Bad guys in jail, lawyers' pockets full, and his Chief one very happy man.

Off to his left, the Pacific Ocean sparkled a deep jade as the sun touched the horizon. With all the windows down, he could smell the salt air, could almost hear each individual wave as it hit the shore.

*Home,* he thought again with a rueful smile. Once upon a time, he hadn't been able to get out of the small, sleepy town fast enough. There hadn't been enough excitement and thrills to be had, but for now, while he was healing, slow and lazy was exactly the speed he craved.

Maybe after he'd slept for a few days he'd test

his still-sore side and go surfing, something he hadn't done in years.

One thing he *didn't* have to do was work, not for one more week, when his leave time would be up. He'd already had nearly two months off, but he could drag it out even longer if he needed; everyone would understand. Being shot took a lot out of a cop.

But Zach loved his work, and wanted to get back to it. It was his life. His *only* life, he admitted ruefully, given the hours and energy he put into it. Besides, the wild, hustling, packed L.A. still gave him a rush.

At the moment though, even his bones hurt, and he had to wonder if he'd really be ready to go back so soon. A ruptured liver and two shattered ribs were harder to get over than he'd even imagined.

Maybe he was just tired. In fact, his eyes were so gritty he could hardly see, and just concentrating on driving was almost more than he could handle. All he wanted right now was a good meal and a bed.

Actually, skip the food, he'd head straight for the sheets, with or without the warm female body.

The Norfolk Woods Inn sign finally came into

view, just seconds before the quaint, character-ridden old lodge did. At the sight, a burst of pride went through Zach for what his baby sister and her friends had created. The log cabin itself was beautiful, warm and inviting and cozy—the very thing he'd run from so many years ago.

Alexi. He missed her. They visited too infrequently, and only when she made the trip to Los Angeles around his work schedule. It'd be good to see her. She'd give him a room and let him sleep around the clock, the entire week if he felt like it. He could contemplate the cosmos, catch up on television.

Hell, he could watch the grass grow.

After the life he'd led for the past year, it sounded decadent. Slow. Leisurely. That it was the opposite of everything he'd ever wanted didn't escape him, but for now it was perfect.

As he pulled up, half dead on his feet, he realized that things were not going to go quite as planned.

The No Vacancy sign was lit.

# 1

BUSINESS AMONG FRIENDS was rumored to be a bad idea. Before today, Hannah Novak would have denied this, but now, in her third attempt to bring order to a very important goal-setting meeting, she had to wonder. "Come on, guys. Let's do this."

Alexi, her best friend and business partner, nodded and bit back her laughter. "You're right, let's get serious."

"Only if we have to." Tara, second-best friend and also business partner, sighed dramatically.

"We have to." Hannah was their voice of reason. She had been since childhood. She couldn't help herself. She liked order, liked a good plan. She had one for every aspect of her life…well, except for the romantic part.

Much to her private vexation, she'd failed miserably there.

"Okay, then." Alexi sent her an innocent smile, which should have immediately raised Hannah's suspicions. "The goal for this summer is to lose our single status." Grinning, she held her pen poised above the pad balanced on her knees. "Correct?"

Tara laughed. "Oh, definitely correct."

Hannah groaned. Lose her single status? In twenty-four years she hadn't managed to lose so much as her virginity. "No. This is not our goal—"

"At least get one really good date," Tara decided. "With a *rich* guy. Yeah, now *there* would be a nice change."

"I'd settle for him being employed," Alexi muttered.

Hannah would settle for having any other conversation. She loved her friends, loved them as if they were sisters, but she didn't want to talk about her pathetic lack of dates. "Hey, what happened to our *business* goals? You remember, the Norfolk Woods Inn? The lodge we run?" It was their pride and joy. It'd been their dream ever since Tara had inherited it right out of high school. "We're going to maybe add on a room, buy new dishes for the kitchen, give the staff a raise...that sort of thing?"

"Nah, catching a man is far more important." Tara fluffed her perfectly sculptured chin-length blond hair. "Three of them to be exact, one for each of us."

"Absolutely." Alexi shoved her own darker, longer, unruly curls out of her eyes and grinned, reminding Hannah that she wasn't nicknamed Rebel Junior—her brother was the original rebel—for nothing. "Men. Pronto."

Hannah tried again, because honestly, catching a man was completely out of her realm of expertise, and they really needed to have this business meeting. "Look, the lodge is completely full, *more* than full, and we only have a little while here. We really need to—"

"I know. *I know,*" Tara said mournfully. "It's just that I'm in the mood for a good romance, that's all." If Alexi was the rebel, then the willowy and elegant Tara was easily the sophisticate of the group.

Which left the goody two-shoes position for herself, and Hannah filled it all too well. "No thanks on the romance. It's too...complicated."

The understatement of the year.

"Complicated, yes. But lots of fun." Alexi looked to Tara for support. "Right?"

Wrong.

For Hannah, romance was too much work to be anything other than agonizing. From the beginning she'd been hopeless at it. Maybe it had been her home life, so different from all her mostly upper-class fellow students. Maybe it had been her own shyness. Whatever the reason, it had started in sixth grade, when she first became truly aware of boys. Fool that she was, she'd fallen hard for Alexi's older brother, Zach, and it had been nothing but humiliating because he thought she was the dreaded "cute."

No boy her age had compared to him, but she'd given it a try. In seventh grade she'd nearly drowned Eddie Bachman in the pool during swimming class because he'd tried to kiss her and she'd panicked.

In eighth grade she'd given Peter Horn a black eye when she accidentally fell on him as he tried to maneuver her beneath the mistletoe during a Christmas dance.

By the time she'd *wanted* a boy to make a move on her, she'd garnered the reputation of hurting any male unfortunate enough to give her a second glance.

The bad rap had stuck.

She'd had dates since then, but exactly one per guy. Just enough to warn them their life was in dire danger if they dared ask her out a second time.

She'd never figured out why she was such a big klutz around men. Her brother Michael said it was because she spent too much of her time worrying about things other kids didn't have to, things like having enough money to eat that week. Or was their mother depressed again. Michael said as a result of those worries, Hannah spent too much time caring about everyone other than herself. But she couldn't help it, it was a habit years in the making.

Hannah believed her brother. She just didn't know what to do about it. Rather than face the humiliation of continuing to try, she'd taken a break from actively pursuing a dating life.

But her heart had never gotten the message. It continued to yearn and burn to know what she was missing.

Which had nothing to do with this meeting, darn it. "Guys, come on now, we—"

"Romance..." Tara said dreamily. "Sweet nothings, slow dancing, and long-stemmed roses. I want the whole enchilada."

"Try a good steamy novel then," Hannah suggested, determined to move on. "They have guaranteed happy endings." She leaned over to tap her pencil on their supposed list of goals, which at the moment included only one—*Lose Single Status.* "We have to get serious here."

But really, who was she to begrudge her friends needing more, just because she'd always failed at it? Just because her whole life was the Norfolk Inn, that didn't mean it had to be the same way for them. Yes, it was a dream come true for all of them to work together at their own business, but neither Alexi nor Tara ever put work ahead of their own personal lives.

Hannah did. She just didn't know how to do anything else.

Maybe they were right. Maybe it was time for a change. A new attitude. She was older, wiser too. Certainly she could do anything she set her mind to.

*After* this meeting.

"So...it's settled?" Alexi asked them. "We're all going for it? Most important goal for the summer, lose single status?"

"Count me in," Tara said. "Hannah?"

"Well—"

"Just third the motion, would you?"

All she had to do was say the words. Put voice to the need deep inside her, that she'd love to find someone to go out with, someone she could trust enough to lose more than her "single" status to.

Besides, Alexi and Tara looked so excited about the prospect of summer, and of finding someone.... How could she disappoint them? She could just agree, and then forget about it. "I give," she said. "Can we finish discussing the business now?"

"How about we up the ante first?" Alexi suggested. "Whoever gets unsingle doesn't have to clean toilets all summer. Seeing as how I'm going to win and all."

"Maybe our goal should be to hire the maid we've been promising ourselves," Hannah suggested instead, but both Tara and Alexi shook their heads.

"We're doing good, but not *that* good, not yet," Tara reminded her. "It's not in the budget until *next* spring."

"So..." Alexi's eyes sparkled. "What do you guys think about the toilet challenge?"

"It's sort of high-school, isn't it?" Tara asked.

Which had Alexi laughing again. "So naturally, you're in."

"Are you kidding?" Tara grinned. "And miss this? Of course I'm in. Like I have to worry about losing anyway."

"Not when we have Hannah in the mix for the handicap."

They both looked at her with warm, loving amusement and she cast a glance heavenward. "Just because I don't date a lot—"

"Honey, you don't date *at all.*"

"Well you wouldn't if you had my bad luck."

"Yes, I would," Alexi said, her face suddenly serious. "I'd try. You just haven't found the right one yet, someone who makes you feel special."

"Absolutely," Tara agreed. "You can't give up."

But Hannah *had* given up. It was far easier on both her heart and ego. "In today's day and age," she said as primly as she could, "we have to be careful."

"Careful yes," Tara corrected. "Alone, no."

"I said I'd do it." And she would, just so they could get on with their work stuff. She didn't want a relationship; she didn't have the time or inclination. And anyway, if she was going to set a goal for herself, it would be something easier.

Something personal.

She wanted to lose her virginity.

"To us then." Alexi held out her hand. Tara placed hers in it, and with reluctance, so did Hannah.

"Good luck, ladies," Alexi said as they shook.

"I declare this meeting concluded. May the best woman win."

"Okay, great." Hannah raised her pad of paper. "Now back to business."

Alexi and Tara sighed but settled in, mostly to humor her. It didn't matter; Hannah was glad to be back on track.

And yet for the next hour, while they discussed finances and services, all she could think about was...what if she'd been too hasty in assuming she would lose their challenge?

What if she could really do it, really actually manage to meet her personal goal of losing her virginity? She could just dip her toe into romance, so to speak, then get back to her life.

Nice dream, but impossible, given reality.

There was no man in sight begging for her body.

HANNAH STOOD ALONE in front of the freshly scrubbed kitchen sink, having just happily run herself ragged cleaning up the evening's meal for their very full house.

Out the window to the right, the sun slowly disappeared over the Pacific Ocean. The colors exploded, and she stood there riveted by the sight.

She loved it here. It was calm, peaceful. Perfect.

To the left, she could see the quaint main street of Avila. All the galleries and specialty shops had their lights on, welcoming. Inviting. Tourists were hustling down the street, shopping, eating, enjoying themselves.

As were their own guests. Their land was only an acre, but it was a fabulous acre, complete with the lodge, a small restaurant, an ice-cream and gift shop, spa, barbecue area, wildflower gardens and eight suites—though they only used five for visiting guests. The other three belonged to Tara, Alexi and herself.

Alexi ran the restaurant with amazing talent for both cooking and charming the guests out of huge tips. Tara handled the books with the fierceness of Attila The Hun, and since Hannah had a way with both greenery and sweetness—or so she'd been told—she worked the wildflower gardens and ran the ice-cream and gift shop.

She could think of nowhere else she'd rather be, and was looking forward to the wonderful summer months ahead...unless of course, she was on toilet duty.

Oh God, she'd almost forgotten.

She'd agreed to the unsingle challenge.

A half-hysterical laugh escaped her. It was so

out of her league she might as well wish for a trip to the moon. And anyway, how bad could it be cleaning the bathrooms every single day, for three entire months?

Pretty bad.

Darn, she needed a man. Not just any man either, she wanted him to be kind and sensitive. Passionate. She wanted him to desire her.

That she also wanted him to be an incredible lover went without saying.

Oh, and then she wanted him to go away.

She laughed at herself, and then shrieked in surprise at the shadow of a man behind her.

"Excuse me," he said, coming into the kitchen. "I—"

He broke off abruptly and stared at her in surprise.

She understood perfectly. Her heart was inexplicably in her throat, she could hardly breathe, because she *recognized* that voice, recognized the boy who was now a man. It'd been ten years, but that low, husky tone was indelibly printed in her mind.

Alexi's older brother, Zach Thomas.

The first boy she'd ever had a crush on.

He'd changed, was her first thought. Lord, he'd changed.

Then a grin broke across his face, and she had her second thought—she hadn't realized her toes could really curl.

"Hannah? Is that you?"

"What—what are you doing here?" *Oh gee, wonder why she couldn't catch a man.* But she was truly stunned to see him since only six weeks ago he'd nearly been killed in the line of duty, shot down by some gangbanger.

Alexi had taken the news very hard, and it had been Hannah who held her best friend while she cried during that first agonizing telephone call. "I thought you were still recuperating," she added. "Are you okay? Should you be up and about?"

"Yep to both, especially since I've only one week left on my first vacation in ten years." He grinned again, and it quite simply took her breath.

It was all coming back to her, the horribly humiliating teenage infatuation—which had absolutely *not* been reciprocated. He'd been kind to her, yes, and as she was a friend of his baby sister, he'd also been indulgent and protective.

But other than that, Zach had been far, far out of her reach; too wild, too gorgeous, too everything. Avila had smothered him, he'd hated the tight confines, the lack of adventure.

Which had been everything she loved about the peaceful, sedate town.

Then he'd left her world to become a cop of all things, and they hadn't seen each other since.

Why should they?

He lived the wild, exciting life he'd always wanted and she...she lived hers the way she'd always wanted, with a few exceptions. Okay, one exception—her lack of a love life, which of course brought all sorts of erotic images to mind, images best not thought about at the moment.

Why? Because Zach was standing right in front of her looking a bit wicked, definitely gorgeous, and just a tad dangerous. He was back and her tummy had gone all tight, her toes were still curled and all sorts of currents were racing through erogenous zones she hadn't even known existed.

Because of one simple smile.

Damn Alexi and Tara for putting thoughts of wild sex in her mind.

*Toilets,* she reminded herself. Eleven of them in the inn. They were hers.

"Who knows when I'll have a whole week to myself again," he said, leaning back against the doorjamb and studying her in an openly assessing way. "I've been promising Alexi I'd come ever since the three of you opened this place."

And he'd finally come.

Right now, tonight. Just as she'd decided maybe she should lose her virginity once and for all. At the thought of losing it with this tall, leanly muscled, rugged man she'd once known, she nearly slid to the floor in a boneless mass of jelly.

"It's nice to be here," he said, still smiling, still gorgeous.

Darn him.

"Well, it's nice to have you," she said, meaning it more than he could know. Alexi had been so worried about him, they'd all been. He'd nearly died, yet it seemed so surreal to think of that when he was standing there in the flesh, looking so…so alive. "Are you really okay?" she asked softly.

"Yeah, I'm really okay…or I will be after I sleep for a week." He shook his head as he studied her. "It's hard to believe how long it's been. You've…" His gaze dipped downward slowly, past the ever-so-lovely apron she wore—not!—all the way to her sandals, then slowly back up again. "You've gone and grown up on me, Hannah."

Oh boy. So had he.

He was still big, still powerfully built, standing there with the casualness of someone totally at ease anywhere. There was a toughness to him that reminded her of what he did for a living, an edge that hadn't been there before, a dangerous one, tempered with restraint.

But it was just Zach. She knew him. Or she had. He dressed the same, in a simple polo shirt and faded, soft-looking jeans.

Nothing else looked soft though, not those long, powerful legs or—

A warm flush stole over her and she guiltily jerked her gaze up to meet his, and found herself just as fascinated by what she found there.

His mouth might still be curved in that sexy, slow, lazy smile, but he wasn't amused, not really. In fact, Hannah would have bet her next paycheck that those fine lines fanning out from his baby blues were from exhaustion, maybe even pain. So was the slight slump to his mile-wide shoulders. His dark, silky-looking hair was on the wrong side of long, curling over his collar, and disheveled, as if he'd run his fingers through it often.

But it was the faint shadows beneath his eyes that grabbed her, and the tense way he held himself in spite of his smile, as if he were close to keeling over. He didn't look like the decorated cop she knew he was. He looked tired, almost brooding, and unsettled.

"Are you sure you're okay?"

Confirming her suspicions, he yawned. "I'm just really beat," he said simply, rubbing a hand over his face. "Long drive, long day. Six weeks out of commission and I'm out of shape."

He didn't look out of shape to her, not then, and not now when he stretched, the movement slow and unconsciously sensual. Hannah found her gaze glued to all those long limbs and fabulous muscles, her mouth suddenly dry.

"I really need a bed," he told her.

Unbidden images flashed through her mind; silk sheets, bare, hot skin pressed against more bare, hot skin; long, drugging kisses... Oh my.

Could she really do it? Could she really make love with him?

As he stretched again, he let out a low, rough sound from deep in his throat.

Oh yeah. She could. Definitely. "Um... Does Alexi know you're here?" An idea stirred, formed. "Never mind," she said. "Just sit." Gently, she pressed him into a chair, her hands burning from just touching his broad, exhausted shoulders, her mind racing with the possibilities. "I'll go get you a room."

"Sounds good."

She hoped he still felt that way in a few moments, because no matter whose brother he was, there wasn't a room to be had.

Which brought her to her plan. Her crazy plan. Her how-to-get-un-virginal plan.

# 2

SO BONE-WEARY he could hardly climb the stairs, Zach shouldered his duffel bag and headed toward the room Hannah had just given him.

Hannah.

It'd been ten years since he'd set sight on her, a very long time given she'd been fourteen when he'd left. Fourteen and gangly and awkward, terribly self-conscious in a way that to his own nineteen years had seemed...well, very young.

Still, whenever he'd thought of Avila, a small part of him had always wondered if she'd kept that sweet smile, if she still had freckles dancing across her nose, if she'd ever grown into her long, skinny legs.

If he wasn't so tired, he might have acknowledged that he now had the answers to those burning questions.

Yes, she still had that sweet, contagious smile, the one that made her green eyes shine like jade.

Yes, she still had a scattering of freckles dancing across her nose.

And most definitely yes, she'd grown into those long, long legs—legs that now could be registered as a lethal weapon, for she'd nearly stopped him in his tracks when he'd stumbled across her in the kitchen.

If he hadn't been about to fall asleep on his feet, he might have been able to fully appreciate those unexpected, and delightful, changes.

He might have even enjoyed the décor of the lodge, knowing his sister and her friends were far more talented than he could have imagined. He might have wondered who Hannah had kicked out of the clearly full lodge in order to give him a place to crash.

But his mind had gone fuzzy, and amazing as it seemed for a man who hadn't been with a woman for far too long, he couldn't even think about it.

He needed sleep.

Beyond that, he probably needed some good food, too, and some serious brain rest, but if he didn't take care of the sleep first, he was going to fall down on the spot.

Again, his job's fault. Portraying someone else for an entire year on the undercover sting, then living on the edge for that long, always on guard and never being able to relax, was incredibly hard on the body.

Oh yes, and being shot.

That hadn't helped, either.

He'd assumed he'd fully recuperate, but suddenly he had his doubts, and it scared him.

His job was his life. He hadn't set out for it to be so, but he'd always wanted to be the best, and to do that, sacrifices had been made. His personal life, for one. He'd been so busy being a cop, being a *good* cop, he'd lost a part of himself. Strange how he'd been perfectly happy that way, until he couldn't do his job.

Now, that life seemed...empty. No, that wasn't right.

Maybe it was just exhaustion.

On the second-floor landing he came to a small sitting area. There was a fireplace, and several couches were nicely arranged for easy gathering.

Seated there was an older couple sharing a pot of tea. *Mr. and Mrs. Schwartz,* they were all too happy to tell him, when he made the mistake of pausing one second too long and they introduced themselves.

Mr. Schwartz gave him a sly smile. "You're here to pick up babes, I bet. Saw a bunch on the beach today."

Mrs. Schwartz turned on him. "You said you didn't notice!"

"Only helping out the young man, dear."

"Did he ask you for help? No!" Mrs. Schwartz took her husband's cup of tea right out of his hands and placed it on the tray in front of them. "Always butting in, you are. I'm sure this nice young man doesn't need any help finding a woman to keep his bed warm at night, especially from you. Isn't that right?"

She looked at Zach questioningly, and under different circumstances, such as when he wasn't literally ready to fall on his face, he might have laughed. "I'm just here to rest," he said, earning a smirk from the older man.

"Well, just 'rest' on the east end," Mr. Schwartz suggested. "That beach is a hot spot. A regular babe magnet."

Mrs. Schwartz smacked her husband.

"Uh...thanks." Zach backed away just in time to see the older man lay the charm on his wife, who cackled her surrender and kissed him.

Shaking his head at the mysteries of a relationship that old, yet still together no matter how rocky, Zach kept walking. His room was at the very far end, down a hallway and away from any activity.

A Good Thing.

He let himself in. Without bothering to turn on the lights, he dropped his bag to the floor and kicked off his shoes. Hannah had told him there was one bedroom, a bathroom and a small sitting room. All he needed at the moment was the bed, so that's where he headed.

The bedroom windows were open to the night air and moon. He'd showered in his condo in Los Angeles before he'd started the drive, so he simply pulled off his shirt, kicked off his jeans, sighed deeply, and slid under the covers.

Before his head settled on the pillow—which held an oddly arousing scent of some sort of flower he couldn't quite place—he was fast and deeply asleep.

HANNAH COULDN'T CONCENTRATE on work, and was it any wonder? Zach was here. *Here.*

It had to be Fate.

Now all she had to do was get him to want to sleep with her. Maybe not a problem for most women, but Hannah knew it would be a task. Never in her life had she been able to make a man want to sleep with her, so she had no idea what made her think she could do it now, but she was up for the challenge.

She had to be. The timing was right, she could feel it. It would help if she knew exactly how to do it, but if she knew what she was doing, then she wouldn't be in this situation in the first place.

Seduce him. That's all.

Zach didn't have to know all her problems. That she scared men off more quickly than she could blink. That she wanted, *needed,* to know what she was missing. No, he could remain oblivious.

It was all perfect, Zach was perfect. Yes, he'd been a wild rebel in his day, but he'd turned out okay. He was a cop, for God's sake. She knew beneath his tough exterior that he was kind. Sensitive.

And as for the passionate part, one look in his eyes and her knees had trembled. That was passion, right? She was fairly certain.

*Just do it.* The slogan worked for running shoes and it would work here. Which was why she'd taken such drastic measures. She'd actually put him in *her* room for the night.

Oh, and one minor detail—she hadn't told him. How else to get him into her bed? How she'd gotten the nerve, she'd never know, but the wheels were in motion now. Zach was in her room, her bed, hopefully exhausted enough to not question it.

To combat the nerves, and to give herself some time to relax, she threw herself into work. She decided to take the late evening shift at the ice-cream and gift shop, and if she was distracted, it was no wonder.

There was a man in her bed.

"Hey, Boss," Karrie called out when she walked in.

Karrie was one of their four part-time employees. She had green hair, green eye shadow and matching green fingernails. She had a silver tongue stud and a pierced eyebrow. And she was absolutely great with the guests.

"I came to help with the crowd," Hannah told her, moving behind the counter.

Karrie looked around her at the nearly empty shop—there was only one young couple in a booth sharing pie—tucked her tongue in her cheek and nodded gamely. "Yeah, I'm pretty overwhelmed here."

Hannah ignored her and used the excuse of being there to devour a triple-decker chocolate cone.

"Ah, you've got *man* trouble." Karrie, all of

nineteen, nodded again, as if she knew all about such things.

"I do not have man trouble. This..." Hannah gestured to her nearly eaten cone. "This has nothing to do with a man." *Not much anyway.* She helped herself to another scoop.

"Whatever you say, boss."

"It really doesn't."

"Uh-huh." Karrie calmly sponged down the counter. "Is he at least cute?"

*Gorgeous.* "I don't know what you're talking about."

"That means yes."

Hannah stopped eating and looked at Karrie with renewed interest. Desperate times, desperate measures, she thought. "Do you...know a lot about men?"

That got a good laugh. "I know about as much as it's possible to know about an alien species."

"So...you know how to..." Oh, this was ridiculous. Embarrassing. Stupid. "Never mind."

"You can't stop there! Do I know how to...what? Snag a guy?"

"No. Um, seduce one."

Karrie grinned. "That's simple."

"It is?"

"Sure. All men are really just one big walking

hormone. If they even so much as sense they're going to get lucky, your job is as good as done."

It had never worked that way for Hannah before, but then again, maybe she'd never made a man feel lucky. "It can't be that simple."

At the giggle behind her, Hannah turned around. The young couple sharing pie were listening with avid curiosity. They were in their midtwenties and were both so pretty they could have walked right out of the pages of *Cosmopolitan.*

"It's really that simple," the young woman said to Hannah.

The young man blushed from chin to roots, and that had his girlfriend giggling again. "Honest."

Hannah shook her head. "Maybe for you. But I've never turned a man into a...hormone before."

"No, it isn't about beauty," the young woman insisted. "It's about how you make *them* feel."

"I can't believe it's that simple."

Karrie looked at her pityingly. "Trust me, it is. Look, flash some skin. Then kiss him, anywhere. Mouth, neck, ear, you pick."

"Then what?"

"Then flash some more skin. It's as good as done, guarantee it."

Hannah turned to the young woman. "Really?"

She nodded emphatically while her boyfriend blushed all the more.

Hmm. It was worth a shot. She grabbed a tablet from the counter and started writing.

Step one: flash skin.

Step two: kiss him. Anywhere.

Step three: more skin.

Sounded easy.

Contemplating her strategy, Hannah spent the rest of the shift working on their stock, even getting her replacement order ready for the following week. She scrubbed the floors. She dusted. *Dusted,* for God's sake.

But she drew the line at cleaning the bathroom. It was Tara's turn. If she failed at this unsingle thing, it would be her turn soon enough.

*Flash skin. Kiss. More skin.*

How difficult was that? From beneath her nerves came something else, something more base. Her insides tingled, heated. The shock wasn't her excitement, but that she felt it at all. For years she'd made sure she was too busy for this romance stuff, mostly to save her pride, but also out of a fear of the unknown. She'd stifled and ignored her own sexuality.

She couldn't any longer. Fact was, Zach Thomas had turned out pretty darned amazing. And he was in her bed, maybe not waiting for her exactly, but he was there nevertheless.

Studying her notes, she went back to the lodge and climbed the stairs. Anticipation raced through her as each footstep brought her closer.

*Men are all one big walking hormone.*

She could only hope that was true, though the mental image of that nearly made her laugh out loud.

She let herself into her little suite. No lights. Good. Not being able to see might help her nerves.

Zach was there, in her bed, fast asleep if his even, deep breathing was any indication. In the dark, she moved closer, peering at him. She could see his head, and one bare shoulder as it gleamed in the moonlight.

Her heart raced, and she promptly forgot everything she was supposed to do.

What first? Squinting in the dark, she reread her notes.

Flash some skin.

Okay, easy enough.

She stripped, trying not to think about the actual technicalities of what she was about to do. Blessing the dark, she dropped shoes, pants, blouse...oh darn. She paused, her hands ready to remove the thin camisole she'd worn beneath her blouse.

Laundry.

She'd forgotten to do it—again.

Knowing she had no nightie in her drawer, not even a clean T-shirt thanks to her forgetfulness, she left on the little silk camisole and hoped it looked sexy enough. To ensure that, she removed the bra she'd worn beneath it. Then she drew a deep, very shaky breath and glanced through the dark at her faint reflection in the mirror over her dresser.

She'd never been one to sleep in the nude, she'd never even slept in just a little chemise and panties before. She felt...sexy. She even *looked* sexy, if the hardly-there reflection told the truth.

She'd always been fairly curvy. Blessed with breasts, as Alexi was fond of saying. But her chestnut-colored hair had always been difficult. Wild at best. At least it fell past her shoulders, which made it easy to pull back when she wanted. For now she left it down, because guys liked long hair.

Or so she'd heard.

Hoping that was true, she attempted to tame it, but it refused to be browbeaten. She couldn't see her eyes in the faint light, but that only added to the strange allure of standing there half nude staring at herself.

In spite of her hair, she really did look good! It was a horribly embarrassing thing to admit, even to herself, but she couldn't tear her gaze away.

An achiness filled her, especially in those erogenous spots that had been tingling ever since she'd first seen Zach again. Now goose bumps rose on her skin as well, and she shivered, though she wasn't cold. The opposite actually.

This was the new millennium. The age of the woman. She was perfectly capable of sleeping with someone, even making the first move if she had to. There certainly didn't have to be any *commitment* involved.

She could do this. She *wanted* to do this. And it had nothing to do with any silly challenge, and everything to do with what she wanted for herself.

Standing there in the dark, she ran her hands down her arms, soothing away the slight tremor that had danced through her with all the racy thoughts. Even that simple touch seemed sensual, and her body tightened. Her nipples puckered.

And she laughed silently at herself. There was a man in her bed; a warm, hard-bodied, sexy man and she was standing here wasting good time.

Zach was utterly still, completely asleep, on his side facing her. So exhausted. A flash of guilt hit her. Should she let him sleep awhile longer?

No. She'd lose her nerve.

It was too dark to see him clearly. Probably a good thing. Dragging in a deep breath of courage, she lifted the covers and slid in. Oh...my, he felt so absolutely wonderful—

All thought deserted her as two large hands caught her, hands which hauled her close, then rolled her, so that she was pinned beneath him and rendered completely immobile.

# 3

A GROAN RUMBLED from Zach's chest, in the region of Hannah's ear.

"What the—" Towering over her, his hands now flat on either side of her head, the length of him became flush with the length of her. Then one of his hands smoothed back the hair from her face. Bending close, he struggled to see in the dark. *"Hannah?"*

Oh God, what now? At the first feel of him, her plan had escaped her. Oh yes, *flash skin.* Thinking she needed to remove her camisole, she started to wiggle, but he held her utterly captive.

One of his hands tipped her face up. "Why are you in my bed?"

"It's...my bed."

"No...this is my bed." He spoke slowly, thickly, as if he wasn't quite awake. "Or at least the one that you gave me. I think. Am I in the wrong bed?"

No, he was in the exactly right bed. And now

that her initial nerves had worn off, Hannah was becoming aware of several things.

One, he smelled good. *Really* good, like soap and sleepy warm, male skin.

Two, he felt good. Really, *really* good. All sleek skin and tough muscle.

And oh yeah, as far as she could tell, he was nearly naked. To test, she arched up, just a little, because wow, he felt incredible. She wasn't really trying to take advantage of him, at least not until he woke all the way up—okay, maybe she was, just a little—and when she did, she encountered...yep, more sleek skin and tough muscle.

No clothes.

At her movement, he'd gone completely still. She could feel him becoming more...*awake*.

Abruptly, he rolled off her.

Shoot! She hadn't moved to step two quick enough! *Flash skin, then kiss him.*

She needed to kiss him in order to render him a walking, talking sex hormone!

But then she was suddenly blinking at the lamp he flipped on.

He was glaring at her. "*Hannah?*"

Hadn't they already established that it was indeed her?

She opened her mouth to say yes, it was *still*

her, but then she realized he was holding his side. "Oh God, did I hurt you?" Horrified, and angry that she could have forgotten about his side, even for a second, she rolled toward him.

"No, I just moved wrong," he said, straightening gingerly, giving her a good look at his scar, which was at least six inches long, red and angry.

Her heart squeezed. "Oh, Zach. I'm so sorry."

"I'm fine," he said roughly.

Yeah, he was fine. Actually, *amazing* was a better word. And still nude. The sheet had fallen away from his chest, pooling low in his lap. Those shoulders she'd admired earlier were no longer slightly slumped with exhaustion, they were straight and quite frankly, mighty impressive.

Not that she'd seen many to compare by, but she had a good imagination.

His arms were long, tanned and solid muscle.

But it was his stomach that really grabbed her. Solid as a rock and rippled, all the way down to…

With a low, inarticulate sound, he hauled the sheets closer to himself and frowned at her.

Blushing, she looked away quickly. Nope, she wouldn't have trouble finding a spot to kiss. If she even got a chance, that is. Seems her bad luck streak hadn't changed much since high school.

Zach blinked at the clock and let out a soft oath as he ran a hand over his face. "What's going on here?"

"I'm..." *Trying to seduce you, darn it!* "Actually, this is my room."

He was still confused. "Because you were sold out and you didn't want to turn me away?"

*No, because I wanted to jump your bones.* "Um...not exactly."

"The No Vacancy sign was blinking when I drove up, but I didn't think—" He swore. "I'm sorry." With a disgusted shake of his head, he rose from the bed.

Hannah, who just a moment ago had been ogling him, squeaked in shock and covered her eyes. He was *very* naked.

"Hannah?"

She kept her eyes firmly covered as he rustled about. "Yes?"

"It's safe."

Oh, some seducer she was. From between her fingers, she stole a peek. Indeed, he'd pulled on his jeans, though he hadn't snapped them yet. He was standing there, looking rumpled, tired, edgy and deeply annoyed.

Not to mention so stunning she could hardly breathe.

It occurred to her that he was now staring at her, *really* staring at her, in a way that made her start tingling all over again.

In all the excitement, she'd completely forgotten her own state of undress. He sounded a little unraveled when he said, "You'd better get covered, too."

Laughing nervously, she grabbed the sheet and wrapped herself in it, wondering if it was too late to get back on task, wondering how to get close enough to kiss him.

"I'll gather my things," he said. "I'll sleep downstairs somewhere until morning."

"No, that's—"

"Yes." His voice was suspiciously husky. His eyes were dark, his mouth grim, and he purposely avoided looking at her. "I'd better go now. Um...Hannah?" He sounded hard pressed for air as she got out of the bed. "The sheet, it's not quite covering..."

She craned her neck and saw that he was right, she hadn't managed to cover her backside. She was giving him quite a show of panties, which never seemed to stay in place. "Oh!" Grace under pressure. She had no choice. She jerked the sheet around her and took a step toward the bathroom where she would hopefully disappear into thin air.

But true to form, she tripped and fell flat on her face.

Zach rushed around the bed, and before she could so much as take a breath, she was scooped against that wonderfully hard, sleek chest she'd so admired.

"You okay?"

Aside from being a bumbling idiot...yeah, she was just dandy. "I'm fine."

"Okay, then." And he withdrew those arms, though his gaze lingered a bit where the sheet dipped down, revealing the top of her lacy chemise. "I'm sorry about intruding," he said.

"It's not your fault." She stared at his jaw which was almost within reach of her mouth. If she could just lean in and connect...

But he turned his head away so that he was no longer looking at her. "I was really asleep," he said. "Really out of it."

She could see that was true, his exhaustion was palpable, and guilt filled her. "I know." She felt a twinge of shame at her deception, and at not being totally honest with him. "This isn't the way our guests are usually treated."

He looked at her then, his gaze filled with all the heat and longing she'd hoped for.

She'd done it!

Then he let her go and stood. "I don't exactly feel mistreated." With a tight smile, he walked out of the bedroom.

"BE HOME, BE HOME," Hannah prayed silently, huddling on the edge of her bathtub, gripping her cordless phone close to her ear.

Her other ear strained for any hint of movement beyond the bathroom door, which she'd shut herself behind for a moment of privacy.

She had no idea what Zach was doing out there, but she certainly didn't want him to hear this.

"What?" came the very welcome, very irritated sound of her brother's voice.

"Thank God you're there," she whispered into the phone.

"Of course I'm here, it's three in the morning on this side of the country. "What's the matter? You okay?"

"I'm fine. I need...information."

"Now?"

She glanced at the closed door, behind which

was Zach, sexiest man on earth, wearing nothing but jeans and attitude. "Right now."

"Okay, make it good. I have to work at six. As in three hours."

"It's...about..." She let out a long breath. "This is difficult."

Michael was a few years older than her. He'd gone to school with Zach. They'd been fast friends, and together had caused more than a few mothers to bite their nails to the quick. If anyone knew how to create a seduction, it would be Michael. "Listen, I need to know how to..." *Just say it.* "Seduce a man."

Utter silence.

"Michael?"

"I couldn't possibly have heard you correctly."

"I think you probably did."

He swore. "Okay, let's pretend it's perfectly normal for you to ask that of me, I'd like to know *why* you want to seduce someone. Now. After snubbing your nose at men for years."

"Because I've matured?"

"You've always been mature."

"Okay, then because I just realized what I was missing."

"Hannah. Seriously. Why?"

"Isn't that obvious?"

"Humor me."

She sighed and took another glance at the closed door, hoping Zach couldn't hear her. "I don't want to be a virgin anymore," she whispered.

*There.* She'd said it. "Now will you help me or not?"

"Hannah—" He swore again, and she imagined him sitting up in bed, hair as wild as hers, frustrated because he couldn't strangle her. "Why are you doing this to me?"

"So you don't know how to do it either." Disappointment hit her like a wave. Now what?

A choked sound came over the phone. "Oh, I know how to seduce someone," Michael assured her. "I'm just not sure I want *you* to know."

"Karrie told me all I have to do is flash skin, then kiss him, then flash more skin. That's all. But it didn't quite work, and now I'm wondering if—"

"Wait a second. Back the train up. You flashed some guy skin?"

"I tried," she admitted miserably.

"Who, Hannah?" He sounded tense. "Who is this you're attempting to seduce? And why now, all of a sudden, are you tired of being a…a—"

"A *virgin,*" she hissed. "See? You can't even

say it, you must understand why I don't want to *be* it!"

"Okay, look. I've got some time coming. I'll fly in for the weekend, we can talk—"

"No!" God, that was the last thing she needed right now, her big brother going all big brother on her. "Can't you just tell me where I went wrong?"

"Hannah—"

"*Please*, Michael," she whispered, suddenly, ridiculously close to tears. "I have to do this. I *want* to do this. I just need a…a tip. That's all."

He let out a long, slow breath. "I can be there in a few days—"

"No."

"I want to discuss this with you—"

"No. Either give me a tip or go back to bed."

"Use a condom," he said through his teeth. "Promise me."

"Done."

"Okay. What Karrie said." He sounded strained. "It should work. God. I can't believe I'm telling you this, but despite what women think, we…men like a little romance too. Music, candles… Dammit, this is so stupid—"

"No, it isn't!" Excitement and renewed hope

filled her. "I have candles—" She broke off at the knock at the bathroom door.

Then came Zach's low, unbearably sexy voice. "Hannah?"

"Thanks, Michael," she said quickly. "I've got to go."

"Hannah, wait—"

"Love you." She disconnected, stared at the door, chewing on her bottom lip.

Romance. Music. Candles.

She could do that.

# 4

"I CAN'T LET YOU sleep on your own couch," Zach said firmly, for the third time. "Take your bed. I'll be fine downstairs."

"Oh, Zach. No. Not when this is all my fault. But it's only because I—" Hannah looked at him, her eyes half closed, with soft shadows beneath them. She held herself in a way that told him she was every bit as tired as he was.

No wonder. It was well past midnight and she'd probably been on her feet since early that morning, serving people, running around and taking care of the inn.

"Come on," he said quietly. "Time for sleep."

"Only if you stay here."

"On your couch."

"Yes," she whispered.

Both of them stood in her bedroom, staring at the bed in question, which was still a little mussed from Zach's first attempt at sleeping.

It was a vivid reminder of how Hannah had

slid into it with him, how he'd come fully awake with her sprawled beneath him, locked in his arms.

She was dressed now, having hastily thrown her clothes back on, but she hadn't been dressed then, and he knew he'd never forget how she'd looked wearing nothing but a few scraps of silk. Or the way she'd looked at *him*, devouring him with her eyes as if she'd never seen anything like him.

It'd been a long time since he'd felt that hard, fast shock of arousal, but he'd certainly felt it then, even as out of it as he'd been.

Hell, he *still* felt it.

Quickly, he glanced at her, wondering if she had any of the same thoughts racing through her mind.

It was hard to tell, since she wouldn't meet his gaze no matter how he craned his neck.

Unfortunately, he wasn't very in tune to women, at least at the moment. Living undercover as he had, within a tough crowd of gang-bangers and basically the scum of the earth, he hadn't even been in close proximity to a woman in a long time.

Too long to possibly guess how to handle this.

"Are you sure?" he asked. "I don't mind going downstairs."

"I'm positive." She flashed him a shaky smile, and moved over to her dresser. With a smile still pasted on her face, she lit a match and held it to the first of three candles she had there. "I mean we're both adults, right?" She lit the second candle, then shot him another smile. "There's no reason we can't both—Ouch!" She dropped the now burned-out match and brought her fingers to her mouth. "It's nothing," she said before he could move toward her. "Do you like candles, Zach?"

Zach figured he must have missed something in his exhaustion, because he definitely hadn't followed her train of thought from the bed to candles. But there was no missing her nervousness. He lifted her chin with his fingers, planning on gently telling her to relax, that he would take the couch, and she the bed, and they could both get some desperately needed sleep.

But at the feel of her soft skin, the strangest thing happened. Something close to an electric current jolted him, only it wasn't painful. No, it was much worse than that, it was…nice. Warm.

Which made it very dangerous.

He wasn't looking for nice and warm. He

wasn't looking for a woman to stare up at him as Hannah was, with wonder and awareness.

Hell, all he'd been looking for was a bed. Okay, and maybe a woman, but someone else, someone...temporary. Hannah wasn't a temporary woman, she was his sister's friend, a woman who would always be around in some form or another because of that. That didn't equal temporary, not in his book.

But his fingers had a mind of their own, and they liked the feel of her so much they didn't let go, but stroked their way to her jaw and cheek.

Her mouth opened, as if she had to do that just to breathe. His own breathing was suddenly just as challenged. "Tell me to leave," he murmured.

"Stay."

"Hannah—" She didn't, couldn't, understand. He was exhausted, dizzy with it. Add to that the fact that he couldn't get the picture out of his head, the one of her half-naked in his arms, which meant he was still aroused. It was wrong.

Eyes lit with something he didn't understand, she moved across the room and hit the power button on her portable stereo.

Soft jazz filled the room.

Then she stared at him, as if waiting for some reaction.

"What about my sister's room?" he asked desperately. He couldn't do this, not with her. "I could—"

"She doesn't have a couch. You know how she is, her room is so spartan."

"Bad timing." The music and candles combined with her expressive, almost hopeful eyes were going to prove too much for him any second now. "*Really* bad timing."

"Oh, Zach. This is all so wrong. I'm trying to...I wanted to...darn it!" She covered her eyes in misery. "I can't imagine what you must have thought of me when I got into bed with you like that."

"There wasn't much thinking involved," he told her honestly. "At first I thought you were just a dream." A really *hot* dream.

"Really?" She dropped her hands from her face and actually looked intrigued!

Letting out a low laugh that released exactly none of his tension, he nodded. "Really. And then when I came all the way awake, and you were beneath me like that, I..."

She licked her lips, probably a nervous habit, but damn if that didn't put the immediacy right back between them.

"I didn't crawl beneath you," she said, her voice husky. Her lips moist from her tongue.

She was close enough to...kiss. *Kiss.* He couldn't get kissing her out of his mind.

"You sorta...put me there," she said softly. "You were confused. My fault." Her voice trembled.

"I scared you. I'm sorry."

"No. No, you don't understand."

He was fascinated by the play of candlelight over her hair. Lightly, he stroked a hand down her back, over her hair, feeling the soft, long strands catch on his work-roughened skin.

"I wasn't afraid of you." It seemed very important to her that he believe her. "I would never be afraid of you."

He was thinking if she could read his thoughts, she might not feel so confident of that. "Because I'm a cop?"

"Because I know you. *Knew* you," she corrected.

"Ten years." He was riveted by the look in her eyes, by the feeling she was waiting for... something, but he didn't know what. "I can't believe it's been so long. You were so young when I last saw you, and now... Look at you, you're beautiful."

"Zach—"

"We never got a chance to say a proper hello, did we?"

"Not a proper one," she said, her lips curving. "No, we didn't."

Slowly, he drew her close. For a brotherly hug.

A nice-to-see-you-again hug.

Big mistake.

His body knew it instantly, at the first shock of holding her against him. *Again.* His mind knew it, too, it was just slower to respond because the feel of her warm, soft curves pretty much blocked out anything else.

"Your side—"

"It's fine," he assured her, and she nodded, tipping her head up, closing her eyes. His body responded automatically, leaning toward her for the kiss—

Wait. No. No kiss. *What was he doing?* With an oath, he pulled away.

She let out a soft sound of disappointment.

This couldn't be happening. He couldn't be wanting her like this. She was his baby sister's best friend. She was his own best friend's baby sister!

And yet the feel of her against him...

"Sleep," he said, far less firmly than he meant, but dammit, he wasn't just a little turned on here.

He was dying.

"Yes, sleep." She cleared her throat and backed away. She glanced at the candles with a sort of...hurt?

He had no idea what that was about.

"I'm going to go downstairs," she said a bit breathlessly. "To get an extra supply of bedding for the couch. Make yourself...at home."

That would be difficult in his current condition. Sleep would be impossible. "Is it all right if I take a shower?" A cold one, a *very* cold one.

"Help yourself." As if she was late for a wildfire, she hightailed it to the door.

He showered quickly, then toweled off, thinking if he didn't lie down soon, he was going to fall down. Eyes gritty, muscles quivering faintly with exhaustion, he hung up the towel and swore.

So used to sleeping in the buff, he hadn't thought to grab clean clothes.

He'd left his bag...where? By the front door. With a huge yawn, he grabbed the towel again, slung it around his hips and tiptoed out, hoping that Hannah had come back and had already fallen asleep.

The lights were off, which he took as a good

sign. She'd gone to sleep then. Making his way in the dark, he tried to be quiet. He tried so hard that he tripped over his own shoes, nearly killing himself in the dark. Pain arched through his side at the sharp movement.

Biting back his oath, he stood again...without his towel, which had fallen. Though the movement was torture, he reached down, searching, but couldn't find the thing anywhere. Finally, he went on without it because he was not only standing there naked as a jaybird, but he was freezing. Feeling for the door, he once again bent down, groping for the bag he'd so thoughtlessly tossed when he'd thought he was in his own room.

As he slung it over his shoulder and carefully straightened, the light came on, blinding him. Lifting a hand up to cover the glare, he heard a gasp.

Hannah's gasp.

She stood by the light switch, still fully dressed. "Okay, this time you scared me," she whispered.

He stood there, stark naked, with Hannah staring at him, eyes huge and dilated, mouth open. "Uh...Hannah?"

"Yes?"

He held his duffel bag in front of him. "Could you cut the light?"

Her gaze was glued to the bag. "You're naked."

No kidding. "I lost my towel in the dark, I forgot my clothes, and...and dammit, why aren't you in bed asleep?"

"I'm not taking the bed, *you're* the guest."

Her eyes hadn't moved from their target, and they were once again filled with that heated awareness. It wouldn't take but a second more of this to completely void out the effects of his cold shower. "Hannah?"

"Hmm?"

"The lights?"

"Oh!" She reached out, then stopped. "If I turn them off, how will you find your way?"

"I'll manage," he assured her through his teeth as he forced a reassuring smile.

"You'll hurt yourself. I'll just close my eyes." Which she promptly did.

"Fine." He hunkered down for his dropped towel, which he could see now thanks to the light, but before he could secure it, her eyes flew open again.

*"Hannah!"*

She bit her lip and looked only slightly remorseful as her gaze once again ate him up. "I just wanted to tell you, the couch is far too small. You'll bump your side or your head all night, or even fall off, or—"

"Okay!" At this point, he was willing to agree to anything if she'd either flip off the light or keep her eyes closed. "The bed then, fine. Just *close your eyes!*"

"Yes! Right!"

Grabbing his towel, he covered himself as best he could, took his duffel and headed toward her bedroom.

The damn woman followed.

"I can find the bed all by myself," he told her.

"I just want to make sure..."

He peered over his shoulder and found her studying his butt. "What are you doing!"

Her gaze jerked up to meet his. Her cheeks reddened. "Nothing!" Guiltily, she scooted back, but remained in the doorway.

He sat on the bed. "You know, I really think I can take it from here."

Nodding, she proceeded to...stay right where she was.

He might have just ignored her, rolling over and falling back into oblivion, but since he'd never in his life taken the easy way, and since she was looking at him with a whole host of things in her eyes, the least of which was a yearning and loneliness that stoked his own, he sighed. "I've got to tell you, the way you're looking at me is going to make sleep impossible."

She swallowed, hard. "You're looking back at me in the same way."

Yeah, he probably was. "Well, how about we both stop. Because if you keep looking at me like that..."

"What?" she whispered. "What will happen?"

"Just stop, okay?" When she only blinked, he rubbed his tired eyes. "It's been a long time since I felt I was in the real world. Back with friends. Back with a woman," he clarified when she just stared at him blankly.

It was a moment before she spoke. "How long is a long time?"

"I can't even remember."

"Well, it couldn't have been longer than it's been for me," she said.

Dangerous conversation. He'd been celibate too long, and now she was admitting the same. After this week, he probably wouldn't get back up here for another couple of years at least, and Hannah meant far too much to him to take advantage of her like that. "Good night," he said softly.

He was both relieved and oddly disappointed when she turned off the light and left him alone.

"CANDLES AND MUSIC didn't work! I need something else, quick!"

Michael let out a long, slow, suffering sigh and yawned loudly in the face of Hannah's hushed panic. "Hannah—"

"Give me just one more tip. Please? I came close," she said quickly before he could hang up. "So close that it should be easier this next time."

"Do I want to know this? No!"

*"Please."*

"Dammit. Okay." He sighed again. "The music and candles failed? Did you combine it with the skin flash and a kiss?"

"Um...not quite. Isn't there some other way?"

"Hannah, this is really awkward—"

"No, it isn't. Pretend I'm...one of the guys. Tell me about your latest conquest. Just do it quick." She didn't have much time, she was close to losing both her nerve and perspective on this whole thing.

Glaring at her closed bathroom door, she huddled on the edge of the tub and sighed. Honestly, she thought she'd had a good shot there for a moment, especially when Zach's eyes had unmistakably glazed over at the sight of her panties.

But she'd lost momentum. Probably when she'd become stupid with lust. Well, no more. She needed to stop wanting to eat him up on the spot and get down to business.

"First of all, it's the middle of the damn night," her bother told her.

As if she didn't know!

"And second of all," he continued. "It's not like I…get a 'conquest' every night of the week."

"So it's difficult for you, too. Maybe it runs in the family?"

He swore again, more colorfully now. "Listen, just tell him. Say, 'I want you'. Have you tried that?"

Well…no, actually. She hadn't.

But she would.

ZACH SUDDENLY CAME AWAKE. He lay there, unsure how much time had passed or what had awakened him. Then came a rustling, the sound of a drawer opening. Blinking his still bleary eyes open into the moonlit room, he saw the slight shadow of Hannah rifling through a drawer.

It was two in the morning.

"Hannah?"

"Oh!" She nearly jerked right out of her skin. Whirling, she put a hand to her chest. "I'm sorry! Did I wake you?"

"What's the matter?"

"L-looking for sweats," she said, her teeth chattering. "I'm frozen."

She wore only a white T-shirt that fell to mid-thigh. Her feet were bare, her arms wrapped tightly around her middle. She looked small and vulnerable. Defenseless. All of which had every protective urge in him out in force.

Damn.

"Come here," he said, and lifted the edge of his covers.

She came, but then hesitated, looking down at him.

"I'm warm," he said gently, thankful she couldn't see how "warm".

"But you told me not to look at you in…*that* way, and if I come in there, I'm going to do exactly that."

Thank God for the dark. "I'll try not to notice. Come on, it's okay."

She slipped into the bed, then lay on her back a bit stiffly. Her teeth rattled, and so did something deep inside him. "Closer. Come on," he coaxed softly, reaching out, touching her hips, urging her on her side facing away from him. Then he scooted her back to his chest so that he could share his body heat. His own exhaustion momentarily forgotten, he stroked a hand down her quivering body, trying to rub some warmth into her.

Gradually, she started to relax, even sighing deeply, snuggling back against him for more heat. "Nice," she murmured.

Until that moment he'd managed to keep his thoughts along the lines of comfort only.

Mostly.

But with her unwittingly seductive voice, and her bottom rubbing over the part of him that had a mind of its own, comfort flew out the window.

It became difficult, if not impossible, to keep his hands on platonic areas of her body. There weren't any! Every part of her drew him, all her long, toned limbs, her sweet, soft lush curves. His fingers stroked down her slim spine, down, down, down... He groaned at the feel of her, unable to keep his hands from exploring.

Another deep sigh escaped her at his touch, and her breath came slow and even.

So he kept on caressing her, trying to keep still,

struggling to hold back another groan because she was heaven in his hands.

"Want you, Zach," she sighed.

He froze. *She wanted him.* Reality reared up and bit him, because while he wanted her back, she couldn't want *him*. She couldn't, this was his own private torture.

Then she sighed his name and whispered it again.

"What?" he asked, praying he'd heard wrong.

Nothing.

"Hannah?"

"Mmm?"

She couldn't just say that and fall asleep... could she? "Um...Hannah?"

This time he got a soft snore for an answer.

*Great.* Her hair tickled his nose, her head was heavy on his arm, making it go numb. Her feet, which felt like icicles, rested on his. Her shirt had ridden up so that the only thing that separated them were silky panties and his own briefs, which were now far too tight for comfort.

He was as hard as a rock, practically shaking with it, and there she lay, peaceful as a baby, getting the sleep that should be his!

It was a long, long time before he followed her into dreamland.

# 5

HANNAH WOKE UP warm and toasty and—*locked in Zach's arms!*

It all came back to her in a flood. The music, the candles…her failure.

Darn it, she'd fallen asleep on him!

Incredible as it seemed, they hadn't done anything.

Hannah would have groaned, loudly, but she was afraid to wake him, afraid to look in his eyes and face her pathetic seduction attempt.

She needed to get up. Needed to regroup. Needed a new plan. But breaking away from the blissfully slumbering Zach was actually harder than she anticipated…mostly because she didn't really want to go. Not when he looked so right in her bed, not when he was wrapped around her making her feel safe and secure.

Wanted.

Whoa. He hadn't wanted her; if he had they would've made love. She needed to remember that when these alien warm and fuzzy feelings came over her.

Zach was here only temporarily.

*Very* temporarily.

Which was yet another thing to remember. No falling for him, no matter how wonderful he felt in her bed.

She made herself get up. Despite her jumbling emotions, her body felt alive, really truly alive, in a way she hadn't imagined possible. Alive and...yearning. She *ached* with it. Ignoring that, she dressed.

When she went down the hall, there was the sweet old couple, Mr. and Mrs. Schwartz, sitting on the couch in front of the fireplace. They were holding hands and talking, and she thought if she could guarantee a relationship like that, then maybe someday she'd give it a shot.

"Get lucky last night, dear?" asked the sweet old lady.

"Ex—excuse me?"

"I saw your young man on his way to bed last night." She winked. "He's something, all tall, dark and attitude-ridden, isn't he?" Then she laughed lustily. "You go, girl."

Hannah managed a weak smile and went downstairs.

Alexi was already in the kitchen, digging through the refrigerator. At the sight of Hannah, a known *un*-morning person, she lifted a curious brow. "Wow. You're even dressed."

"Well, we do have guests," Hannah said, smoothing down her sundress self-consciously because she rarely wore dresses and had no idea why she'd worn one today.

Okay, she did know, but refused to attribute it to Zach. "I could hardly come down in my p.j.'s. Have you met that older couple—"

"Mr. and Mrs. Schwartz. Oh yeah. We had to switch them with another guest, that quiet young woman, Katie Minor. The Schwartzes were...uh, making noises all night, disturbing Mr. and Mrs. Peterman. Can you imagine? They must be at least seventy, right? Anyway, they're in room six now, so they can knock it out all they want, scream at the top of their lungs, swing from the rafters if they like, and they won't be able to disturb anyone."

Hannah shook her head. "Could have done without *that* image this early in the morning, thanks."

"Hmm." Alexi studied her until Hannah squirmed. "My brother snoring?"

"Snoring? Uh...no."

Alexi, who never missed a thing, set down a bowl of fruit and came closer, eyes narrowed. "What's up with that anyway? I would've put him in my room."

*What was up?*

Well, wasn't that just the question of the day?

Hannah could have told Alexi everything. Right then she could have explained that their silly little toilet challenge had started her thinking. That she was feeling inexplicably lonely, even in a lodge completely full of people. That she needed more, needed to know what it was like to share intimacy with someone. That she wanted to know, for once in her life, that she was completely, totally irresistible to a man.

She wanted that man to be Zach Thomas. Strange how much she wanted that, but she couldn't hide from it.

And after last night, she doubted he'd be able to either.

She knew Alexi would have wanted to help Hannah sort this all out, but she didn't share her thoughts.

How could she when she didn't fully understand them herself?

"Hannah?"

"Nothing's up," she said as lightly as she

could. "Just hungry. Can't a girl be hungry first thing in the morning?"

"Yes, but first thing in the morning is not usually before ten for you."

"I'm changing my ways." To prove that, she grabbed an apple out of the bowl and bit in. "Where's Boss?"

Boss was a sixty-five-year-old mislocated cowboy, who just happened to cook with amazing talent. They'd hired him one morning after giving him a handout, and in the nine months since, he'd been a godsend, trading off restaurant duty with Alexi.

"There's a rodeo coming to town, he's all excited. Wanted the day off to go check it out." Alexi didn't take her eyes off Hannah. "And you're changing the subject."

"It worked."

"Okay, fine. Be mysterious. I'll figure it out for myself." Alexi hopped up on the counter, crossed her arms and gave her a long look. "Let's see now...something's different about you...what is it?"

Hannah nearly laughed, but since it would have been a half-hysterical one, she managed to keep it to herself. "Don't be silly. Nothing's different." *Not yet anyway.*

"If I didn't know you better, I'd say that something happened between you and Zach last night."

Yeah, something happened—exactly *nothing!* "But since you *do* know me," Hannah said, surprisingly hurt, "you know that would be ridiculous, right?"

"Right," Alexi said quietly. "Because you're not the type to go for a one-night stand. And while my brother isn't a saint by any means, Mrs. Schwartz said he was nearly unconscious with exhaustion. So that couldn't be it."

Of course not. She wasn't exactly the type of woman to inspire enough wild passion to overcome exhaustion.

But she wanted to be!

Alexi was still watching at her. "Spill it."

"I'm famished." Fishing in the refrigerator, Hannah came up with bagels, cream cheese and a carton of orange juice. "Don't suppose I can convince you to start breakfast early?"

"Don't suppose you can." But Alexi relented with a sigh, hopped off the counter and took out a frying pan. "So...you worried about something?"

Yeah, that she would die a virgin. "Such as?"

"Life," Alexi said in her usual frank manner,

putting bacon to cook on the range and turning back to Hannah with a concerned expression. "You don't enjoy it enough."

Hannah thought about last night and her useless efforts. "That might have changed recently."

"It should. Have you thought about seriously trying to get some fun in your life?"

Now. Now was the time to tell Alexi that she was planning on seducing her brother, that if she was successful, Hannah wouldn't be cleaning toilets this summer.

"Honey, really, there's so much more to life than this lodge."

No kidding. There was love for one thing, an elusive, tricky emotion she knew little about. "I'm working on that fun part."

"Good. You can't live for work alone."

All of Hannah's life she'd pretty much lived for survival. Having lost her father young, it was deeply inbred, especially since she and her brother had spent so many years watching her mother struggle just to feed them. So now maybe she went overboard sometimes, keeping her eyes only on work. But it was a hard habit to break. She intended to try.

The fact remained, though, that regardless of what drove her, Hannah loved the Norfolk Inn. It wasn't a hardship for her to throw herself one hundred percent into the place. Not to mention she actually depended on their earnings for things she'd gotten used to—like eating.

Maybe she had too much pride, she didn't know. But working had certainly gotten her through some tough spots in her life.

Such as when her mother had lost her job. Hannah had been twelve that year, Michael seventeen, and times had been very lean. Instead of going on welfare, they'd all worked, even Hannah, who'd lied about her age and cleaned houses.

They'd survived, only to lose their apartment to a fire a few years later. During it all both Hannah's mother and Michael had managed to retain a sense of themselves, separate from their necessary survival. They played and loved every bit as hard as they worked.

Somehow Hannah hadn't learned the trick of that.

Tara came dancing into the kitchen then, the only one of them a confirmed morning person. She looked perfect as always, every hair in place, impeccably dressed in a fashionable lime-green sleeveless sweater and matching suede miniskirt. She took one look at Alexi's jean shorts, then Hannah's casual sundress, and grimaced. "Have neither of you learned anything from me over the years? Clothes make the woman, ladies. And your clothes won't make anything but the thrift shop."

"Hey, and good morning to you, too," Alexi said cheerfully.

Tara poured herself some coffee, took a grateful sip and moaned with pleasure. "Darling, never mind your clothes. Your coffee will get you into heaven for certain."

"Oh, good. I was so worried." Alexi rolled her eyes and turned back to the range. "Don't you have something more important to do than diss our clothing?"

"Yep." Tara took another happy sip from her mug. "Tons. Oh, and I just saw your brother stagger out of Hannah's room."

Hannah, who'd just taken an unfortunate bite of her apple, choked.

Both Tara and Alexi stared at her odd reaction and she tried gamely to look innocent. "Sorry," she gasped, hitting her chest as the bite burned all the way down. "It went down the wrong pipe."

"I didn't expect him to be up so early," Alexi said with a frown, putting down a spatula. "Did he look okay?"

"Doesn't he always?" Tara sighed dreamily.

"He wasn't wearing much, just a pair of jeans—and please let me break in here and say that man absolutely has the finest looking ass—"

"Hold it!" Alexi looked disgusted. "Jeez, that's my brother you're talking about."

"Sorry." Not looking in the least bit sorry, Tara calmly sipped at her coffee.

"Did he seem...well, still beat half to death?" Alexi was frowning over the stove. "I'm so worried about him, the way he pushes himself."

"He did look beat. A very gorgeous beat I might add." Casually Tara looked at Hannah over her steaming coffee. "He was looking for you, by the way."

Hannah managed, barely, not to choke again. *He was looking for her*. Probably wanting to know what the heck last night had been about. And when she decided how to tell him, she would. Probably. With careful precision, she smoothed her dress and studied her sandals.

"Everything all right?" Tara asked.

"Why wouldn't it be?" Not meeting anyone's gaze, she leaped off the stool she'd been sitting on and headed toward the door. On the off chance he was going to come looking for her, she needed to hightail it out of the kitchen.

She hadn't given up on her goal, not by a long

shot, but she really needed a new plan. "Better run. Got lots of stuff to do."

"But what about your breakfast?" Alexi set down her wooden spoon and eyed her strangely. "You're starving, remember?"

"I just remembered...a thing I have to do."

"What thing?"

"Lots of things. *Tons* of things—" As she whirled to escape, she plowed into a hard wall.

Zach's chest.

"Hey there," he said, steadying her with his big, warm hands, hands she wanted all over her body. "Where's the fire?"

"We were just trying to figure that out ourselves," Alexi said, still eyeing Hannah oddly. "But I'm glad you're here. A room should open up today or tomorrow at the latest. In the meantime you can have my room or the office couch, okay?"

Zach, whose gaze hadn't left Hannah's, nodded. "No problem."

"I've got breakfast going," Alexi said. "Your favorites, on the house, just because. Have a seat."

He couldn't have a seat, though, because Hannah blocked the door. Unless she moved, he couldn't get past her. But she couldn't move, couldn't look at him.

She'd get all hot inside, probably turn red. Maybe start stuttering like an idiot. Dammit, what was the matter with her? This was to have been so simple.

Only ever since she'd first seen him, there hadn't been anything simple about it. Whether she liked it or not, she felt something for him, and yes she'd always felt it, even ten years ago. Only now it was intensified.

"Sorry," she murmured, backing up, giving Zach room to move past her.

But he didn't budge, and oh Lord, he was looking at her with *that* look, the one she'd discovered last night could melt her insides to butter and made her knees weak. "Stop that," she whispered.

"Stop what?" Alexi-the-super-hearing-woman wanted to know. "And why are you just standing there, Zach? I'm not going to serve you way over there."

Zach didn't take his eyes off Hannah. "We should talk, don't you think?"

"Talk?" Tara's eyebrows disappeared into her bangs. "About what?"

"Let me get you something to drink," Hannah

said quickly. She headed toward the counter for a mug. She picked up the pot of coffee, mind racing. What was protocol for this morning-after stuff, because though they hadn't actually done *it*, they *had* slept together, and she was clueless.

Was there some special ritual? Some special code?

She could ask Michael, but she was beginning to think he didn't have a clue about his own species. *Music, candles and a condom?* That was all he'd had to offer? And anyway, she could have figured out the condom part by herself.

She held the mug up to Zach. "Condom?" she asked, then gaped at him, horrified. "I mean coffee! *Coffee!*"

"Wait, did you say…condom?" Alexi asked her in disbelief.

Hannah didn't dare look at her, or at Tara for that matter, who was now bent over, practically rolling with laughter.

*Denial,* she decided quickly. "No," she said with as much dignity as she could muster. "I most definitely did not say…say…*that*."

"Condom?" Tara broke in oh-so-helpfully. "Is that the word you're looking for?"

"I think that's the one," Alexi said, grinning and nodding.

"I did *not* say that word," Hannah said, giving up on dignity because really, after this, there was none to be had.

"Oh, but you did," said Tara with a wide smile. "You most definitely did. Didn't she, Alexi? Say the word condom?"

Zach just looked at the mug, his mouth twitching suspiciously.

Hannah had to hand it to him. Other than that twitch, he remained completely cool, and despite her blunder, some semblance of relief filled her because he wasn't going to add to her misery.

But then he spoke.

"Thanks," he said easily, blowing into the steaming coffee before speaking again. "Oh, and if you don't mind, I'll take it extra large— Er, I mean with sugar."

He shot her an innocent smile while her supposedly best friends roared with laughter.

# 6

ZACH DIDN'T KNOW what to think. He'd come back to Avila to heal, to recover, to regain his strength, and yes, to get his first mental break in far too long.

He'd actually needed the mental break more than he'd thought. Sleeping, eating, healing. More sleeping. This had been his plan.

After a good amount of that, he'd head out of this sleepy town and go back to Los Angeles, refreshed and ready to rock and roll. Ready to take on his job.

No attachments.

But all that had been before last night, and though nothing had happened between him and Hannah—nothing *could* happen between them—it had been a most incredible, erotic night.

Suddenly, he didn't recognize his plan anymore.

He should shrug it—and Hannah—off, just enjoy the rest of this vacation. But he couldn't seem to do that.

For one thing, he was confused about last night and his feelings for Hannah. He'd assumed he'd feel brotherly toward her, but brotherly had been the last thing he'd felt.

Distance. He needed it. To help him get it, he went for a walk through the grounds. The lodge was beautiful, with the cabinlike architecture made famous in the early 1930s. High wood-beam ceilings, log walls, and beautiful, polished hardwood floors. Every room was a masterpiece. The garden, too, with its lush and wild colors, so beautifully bordered by the Pacific Ocean.

It all called to him on some deep level he hadn't expected; the salty breeze, the wide, open beach, the crashing waves. He'd lived here, had grown up here. Back then he couldn't wait to get out. It was all he'd wanted.

So why did it feel so good to be back?

Whatever the reason, he renewed his promise to himself to dig up a surfboard and revisit his wild adolescence.

"Psst."

Zach turned around. Mrs. Schwartz was leading her husband out of the gardens by the hand, though the man was grinning at Zach over his shoulder as he went.

"Don't forget...east end beach!" he whispered conspiratorially.

Zach laughed and waved. "Got it. Thanks for the babe tip."

The older man winked and disappeared out of the garden.

Zach skipped east end beach—wasn't quite in the babe-hunting frame of mind—and found the ice-cream/gift shop. He figured if he was abstaining from babes, he might as well get a cone.

The shop wasn't crowded. He wended his way through to the order counter. To his surprise, he found Hannah on her hands and knees behind it, squinting at a low shelf of what was clearly an inventory closet. Her long, wavy hair fell past her shoulders, and was obviously in her way because she tossed it back with impatience, her face drawn in concentration.

Kneeling next to her was a young woman with startlingly green hair.

"The skin flashing thing...it didn't work," Hannah was saying to her as she foraged into the shelf.

"You're kidding! Are you sure you made it clear what you were trying to do?" the green-haired woman asked. "I mean, men aren't usually that slow."

"So I've heard," Hannah muttered. "Couldn't tell by my ridiculous attempts though." She sat back on her heels and smiled ruefully. "I'm getting ready to pack it in and consider myself a virgin until the end of time."

It was a good thing Zach hadn't gotten his ice cream yet or he'd have swallowed it whole.

"You just need to try again," Green Hair said kindly, patting Hannah's hand. "You're so smart and funny. And pretty, too. Honestly, you'll get it right."

"I'd settle for just getting *it*."

Karrie laughed while Zach forgot to breathe.

"Maybe try another man entirely?" Green Hair suggested.

"I like *this* man."

"Well, try again then."

"A new plan?" Hannah asked hopefully. "I really like a good plan."

They were talking about *him*, Zach realized, stunned.

"Hey, that dress you're wearing is pretty terrific," the young woman told Hannah. "Good, soft material. Very clingy in all the right places. Has he seen you in it yet?"

"This morning, but I didn't exactly get the reaction I wanted."

"Make sure he feels the material, with his fingers. Guys are really into the physical."

The *physical* part of Zach's existence was beginning to make itself known. He just couldn't absorb it all quickly enough. Hannah—a virgin, but not wanting to be a virgin, and not wanting to be one with *him*.

"He needs to touch the dress?" Hannah asked her doubtfully. "Really?"

"Oh yeah. And make sure you send all the right signals while you're doing it. Give him the dreamy eyes and soft sighs and everything."

"That part won't be difficult."

Zach didn't know whether to be flattered, annoyed or stunned. So he settled for all three.

That was the exact moment Hannah caught sight of him. "Oh…" was all she said, blushing. She surged to her feet, tripping awkwardly over the skirt of her dress. "Hey, would you look at that? It's break time already, Karrie."

"But I just got here." Karrie peered at her black, spiked watch.

"Yeah, well, this is National Take-A-Break-Every-Five-Minutes Day. Enjoy it."

"You're making that up."

"Five minutes," Hannah said firmly, still staring at Zach. She continued to stare at him while Karrie left. "Hi."

"Hi back," he said. "I'm not sure what to say."

"Well, that would depend on how much you heard." She looked mortified. "Feel free to lie and tell me you heard nothing."

"I heard everything."

She took that in with a little nod. "And here I thought it couldn't get worse."

A woman in her midtwenties walked by. She didn't have green hair, but was so beautiful, she looked almost unreal. When she saw Hannah, she stopped short and...giggled, ruining the effect.

"So...did any of those tips we gave you work for you last night?" She glanced sideways at Zach, sizing him up.

Hannah looked as if she wanted a hole to open up and swallow her. "Maybe we could discuss this another time," she suggested to the woman.

The woman grinned at Zach. "Sure."

Zach waited until they were alone again. "Let me get this all straight. Last night...you were trying to..."

"Yes," she said miserably. "And to tell you the truth, I'd rather you didn't tell me how ridiculous it was."

"I...wouldn't do that."

"Really?" She smiled a little. "You're awfully kind."

That made him laugh. "Hannah, kind is about the last thing I'm feeling at this moment."

"What are you then?"

*Turned on, dammit.* "I'm not sure."

She thought about that. "Well then, I guess I have nothing to lose...." With that, she moved closer, then closer still, until the skirt of her sundress touched his thighs.

Around them, the air thickened. Her scent came to him, light and pretty. Sensuous. Her eyes were huge, and despite her bold move, very uncertain.

A complete opposition to the way her body swayed toward his. She took his hand in her much smaller one and brought it to...her stomach?

*Make sure he feels it.*

Karrie's words came back to him, and he didn't know whether to laugh or groan. "She was wrong," he whispered, his voice hoarse with the desire he was fighting with his every breath. "It's not the material a man wants to feel."

"No?"

She sounded breathless, too, and in contrast to

his words, his fingers spread wide to touch as much of her as he could, feeling her belly tighten. "No. It's skin I want. Bare skin."

Her mouth formed a perfect little O at that. "I...see."

"Hannah..." She seemed so vulnerable, yet unbearably sexy at the same time, and now that he knew she'd never been with a man, that she was yearning and burning for just that, he could hardly breathe. "What's going on?"

"I thought you already knew."

"I mean other than you're asking your clerk and guests for hints on how to..."

"Seduce you?" She winced. "I asked my brother, too."

"Michael? God." He let out a slow breath. "But why?"

"Why am I asking for tips?"

"Why everything. Why me? Why are you a..."

"Virgin." Her eyes went sad. "It's that awful, huh?"

"No. *No,*" he said again, then shoved his fingers in his hair as if that could help him think. "Hannah...why are you doing this?" *To me,* he wanted to add, but better him than some other guy, right? At least *he* could resist her.

Probably.

Okay, maybe he was going to have trouble in that department.

The phone rang, and he'd never been so relieved in his life.

With a small sound of frustration, Hannah backed away and answered it. Then her shoulders sagged almost imperceptibly, and her smile went tight. "Mom? Everything okay?" She listened intently, and while she did, Zach backed up and pretended interest in a selection of T-shirts to give her some privacy.

He wondered if she'd be insulted if he went running.

Probably, he decided.

"What about the money I sent you last week?" he heard her ask. "No, Mom, Michael paid that bill for you already. The other money we sent was for *you*." She sighed, and when Zach risked a peek at her, she was hunched over on a stool behind the counter, rubbing her temples.

Zach remembered Hannah's mom, vaguely, from their school days. A nice, harried woman in perpetual grief, trying to do it all: work full-time, raise two children on her own, and manage all the household chores that came with that responsibility. She'd always seemed...haggard. Worried. He knew Hannah had grown up hovering near the poverty line, and knew for her mother at least, little had changed.

He was also aware of the fact that Hannah completely depended on her income from the Norfolk Inn, every penny, much more than either Tara or Alexi, both of whom could go to their parents for help if they needed to.

The inn was still fairly new, still earning its reputation. There'd been renovations needed, big ones, and the three women had procured a loan to cover the costs.

Zach couldn't imagine the revenues from the place paid enough to easily support Hannah, much less her mother, not yet anyway.

And damn if that didn't twist at the heart he was trying so valiantly to ignore when it came to the elusive Hannah Novak.

"Don't worry about it, okay, Mom?" Her voice was reassuring in a way one would expect a mother to speak to a child, not the other way around. "Michael and I'll send you more. We'll get it all taken care of.... Gotta go, I have a customer. Yes, I'll call you more often. I love you, too. Bye."

Slowly she hung up the phone, her gaze focused off in the distance as she did, her mind a million miles away. Probably figuring out how to give more, as if she hadn't been giving all her life.

God, she was beautiful, Zach thought, hauntingly so. But it wasn't that physical beauty drawing him now. It was that spirit and inner strength.

*Walk away*, he thought. You're on temporary leave from a demanding job, one that doesn't give you the luxury of letting a woman into your life, even if you wanted, which you don't.

*Just walk away.*

Instead he moved toward her. "Hey," he said softly. "You okay?"

She jerked, then blinked at him once before pasting another of those fake smiles on her face, the kind he was certain fooled any customer because it was such a pretty, friendly smile.

It didn't fool him because it didn't quite meet her eyes, eyes that were filled with mysteries. He'd always known the warm, cheerful, sweet and engaging Hannah had depths to her, but suddenly he wanted to explore them, every single one. Dammit. "How's your mother?"

"She…misses me." Guilt flashed across her face. "I don't spend enough time with her, and whenever she calls I'm reminded of that—not that she bugs me about it or anything—but I can hear the loneliness in her voice. It kills me." Another sigh broke free from her lips, and with everything inside him he wanted to help.

"I hear the same thing when I call my parents," he admitted quietly. "I don't do it enough because of how it makes me feel when I hear how old they sound."

The smile on Hannah's face faded as she absorbed that. "I know. I hate hearing my mother age."

"I worry that I don't see them enough and someday they won't be around to see at all. And Alexi, too. I go too long without seeing her. I've been gone so much in the past years. They hate that."

He hadn't meant to say so much, had meant only to prove kinship with her, but her eyes were deep and clear, and he felt as if he could see himself mirrored there. Certainly his own feelings were reflected back, which shouldn't have surprised him.

Neither should the fact that at that moment, he felt closer to Hannah than he did to anyone.

"Do you miss them when you're working?" she asked.

"When I'm working I don't have time to miss them. It's only now, when I'm off, that I think too much. I can't believe how many years have passed since I've been in Avila."

"Your work is important to you." She gave him a small smile. "And I don't really know much about it."

"I've been doing undercover work." It was his standard, nondescript line. But it wasn't enough for her, and he suddenly didn't want it to be. So for the first time, he expanded on it. "Working on a drug ring in Los Angeles."

"Did you haul them all off to jail?"

"It took a year, but yes, we got them all."

"Good. You're going back into that world soon."

"Yes." He *was* going back. Couldn't wait to be going back.

"It's dangerous," she said quietly, her gaze moving down, landing on his injured side. "Your world."

Suddenly going back was the last thing he wanted to talk about. And just as suddenly, the thought of doing it all over again, becoming someone else, losing another year of his life, maybe two, made him yearn for something... more.

Which made no sense.

He loved L.A. He loved being a cop. He really

did, but he realized he didn't love the way it consumed him. The way it made him feel as though the real Zach didn't exist.

And not for the first time, he considered his devotion to the department, and what it was doing to his own personal life.

It was killing it.

There had to be a better way, a way to have both a life and the job, but he couldn't imagine what that was.

That was fatigue talking, he figured.

"Isn't it?" she pressed, waiting for an answer. "Dangerous?"

"I'm careful," he said finally.

She snorted. "How careful can you be against a punk with a gun?"

"You worry about me," he said with some surprise.

"I worry about lots of things. I worry about the stray cat we have, I worry that the guests won't have enough towels, I worry that—"

"You worry about *me.*"

She went still, then smiled. "Yes. I can't seem to help it. The worrying. Alexi starts it, and then it becomes contagious."

"I love my job, Hannah."

"I know."

He had to shake his head. "We can go on about this and get nowhere. It isn't what I want to know."

"No?"

"No."

Her face went guarded.

"We need to discuss it, Hannah. Last night." He didn't want to, he really didn't. "I won't be able to think about anything else until we do," he admitted.

That brought a new light to her expression. "Really?"

"Did you think I could just forget?"

Before she could give him any answers, the door to the shop opened. Karrie came back in, craning her neck with curiosity. "Break's over," she called out. "Here I come, ready or not."

Hannah blew a strand of hair out of her eyes and shot him a frustrated look. "The timing in my life, in case you hadn't noticed, is really, *really* off."

The strand of silky hair slipped back over her eye, and without thinking about it, or their audience, he gently tugged it back.

She went absolutely still as once again a simple touch seemed to rock both of their worlds. And this time, at least for him, it had nothing to do with the way she filled out her sundress, which happened to be incredible.

It had everything to do with Hannah the person. "We really need to talk," he said quietly.

She bit on her lower lip, but nodded. "I only have a few hours of work to do around here. Some inventory stuff. Then...I'm free for a little while."

*Walk away. Don't get involved.* And yet, he stroked a finger down past her ear, delighting in the shiver that wracked her. "You feel so soft." His thumb brushed her jaw and she let out a soft sigh.

It thrilled and terrified him at the same time, so he pulled back.

She smiled, a bit uncertainly, tugging at his heartstrings yet again, and he found himself returning the smile.

For reasons he didn't come close to understanding, he shifted forward again, meaning only to kiss her cheek once before he left. Except she shifted at the same time, turning her face toward his.

And their lips met.

It was brief, but so warm and innocent. So incredibly right, and filled with unbearable yearning.

Slowly, he straightened.

They stared at each other.

Zach had no idea what it meant, but given her doe-caught-in-the-headlights look, Hannah didn't know, any more than he did. It was the sort of kiss he wasn't likely to forget.

He doubted she would, either.

# 7

THE LODGE WAS BUSY. Summer was in full swing, and as a result, it was more than a few hours before Hannah managed to come up for air.

It hadn't helped that Karrie came down with some sort of flu, turning the same shade of green as her hair, which left Hannah facing the dessert crowd by herself.

It happened to be her specialty, mostly because she loved to eat it. On a normal day, she would have enjoyed serving, enjoyed chatting. She loved to talk to their visitors, learning about them and where they came from.

But today wasn't normal.

Today she had something to do when she was finished, something that wasn't just another chore or more work. Today she had Zach waiting for her, waiting for answers, maybe waiting for more than answers, which is what she'd wanted.

But the reality of it so unnerved her she ate two ice-cream sandwiches.

She had to remember, no matter what happened, that this was just a temporary interlude for Zach, one he'd probably remember with fondness as he went back to his adventurous, exciting life, but he *would* go back.

As if she'd summoned him, he appeared outside the window of the shop, carrying a surfboard and heading toward the beach.

She didn't let herself appease her curiosity by plastering her nose to the full picture window on the side of the shop that faced the beach.

Much.

Near the water, he stripped off his sweatshirt, then his pants, too, leaving him in nothing but swim trunks that clung to his body like a glove.

Had he said he was out of shape? she wondered, pressed up against the window. Not possible, not with that powerful, sleek build. Clearly favoring his right side, he waded into the water and put the board to good use.

"Who are you watching?"

Hannah bumped her nose on the glass. "Nobody. Nothing," she said, turning as casually as she could to face Tara.

"Uh-huh." Tara grabbed a bowl and helped herself to a triple scoop of Fudge Ripple. "Which is why, of course, you're blushing."

Hannah cursed her fair skin as Tara proceeded

to top her dessert with whipped cream. "I always blush."

"It's a good thing, too." Tara paused to moan sinfully as she took her first bite. "Otherwise, how would Alexi and I ever know what's up with you?"

"I tell you what's going on with me."

"The surface stuff maybe, but not the *good* stuff."

"Such as?"

"Such as why you're watching Zach surf while pretending not to."

"Oh. That."

"Would it have anything to do with the curious call I just took from Michael?"

Dammit. "That depends."

"On what? On how badly you freaked him out?"

"That bad, huh?"

"I just barely convinced him not to drop everything so he could come out here and kick *'some stupid jerk's ass'*."

"Oh boy." Hannah let out a disparaging laugh, sank to a chair and looked at Tara helplessly. "You did talk him out of it, right?"

"Yep. Told him I had things under control. Told him Alexi and I would kick any butt that needed kicking. Which means you owe me now. So sing. What's up?"

"Look, I know I've been acting a little strange—"

"A little?"

"But I'm not ready to talk about it."

"You talked to Michael about it."

"Yeah, well, I have a new tactic." She'd figured out it was an individual thing. She had to do this by herself. "And if I'm looking out the window a lot, it's because I'm thinking of what I'm going to change in the garden."

"Right. That explains the dreamy look you had in your eyes. *Flowers.* Silly me, thinking it was that tall, gorgeous cop out there in the water."

"Tara—"

"Honey, look." She set down her ice cream and went serious. "I know you have this misguided thing that because you don't have any money, you think you have to work harder than Alexi or me, but quite honestly, that's a bunch of bologna. Okay? We're all equals, and we help each other. We love each other. So when I see you today, smiling like an idiot, offering a beautiful man a condom instead of coffee, then gazing out the window lost in a daydream, it thrills me. Don't ruin it for me."

Hannah didn't know what to say to that.

"So...what happened last night between you and Zach that's got you acting like a jumping bean? Or should I just guess?"

"No!" Stalling now, Hannah opened the industrial refrigerator and gazed at her stock, eyeing the two huge strawberry pies she'd planned to give to Alexi for the restaurant. Scooping them up, one in each hand, she turned back to Tara. "I'm sorry. I love you, too. With all my heart. But this is something I have to figure out for myself."

"So no more midnight calls to New York?"

"I think I have it handled."

"I'm sure your brother will be happy to know that the birds-and-bees talks are over."

Hannah worked at keeping her expression even.

Tara sighed. "Fine. I'm leaving it alone."

"Good."

"Really. I'm washing my hands of it."

"Great."

"But—"

Hannah gave her a long look, which Tara ignored. "Just remember, it's more than just music and candles. It's all in the body language." She stood and grinned. "Just in case you're wondering." She laughed when Hannah rolled her eyes.

"Hey, don't blame me for prying. Blame Alexi and Michael. I'm not allowed to go back to the lodge until I know what's going on between you and Zach. Michael wants to know if he needs to kill him, and Alexi wants to know if she's cleaning toilets for the summer."

Hannah groaned, and still carrying the pies, she moved through the shop. "We've been out of high school for years, you know."

"I know." Tara smiled. "We really do love you, Hannah."

Well, darned if that didn't effectively defuse any resentment at the unwelcome probing. "Then wait here like a good girl. Answer the phones and feed the guests until I get back."

"Well then, hurry. I'm not done questioning you. I have a feeling whatever it is, it's good. Oh, and don't forget the condom. Michael said to remind you."

"Gee, thanks." Hannah squinted as she entered the bright sunshine, relieved to be out of the spotlight, if only for a moment. She smiled at the Hornsbys, who were kissing madly beneath an oak tree. They were a honeymooning couple who'd been at the inn all week, though they'd rarely surfaced from their room.

They waved at her, and kept on kissing.

She didn't blame them. It was a glorious day. A kissing sort of day. The fog had burned off early, leaving the sun high above, providing a much welcome warmth after their unusually chilly spring.

The lodge looked welcoming. In front of her was the colorful garden she considered a labor of love. Off to her right, the waves hit the shore. Helpless to stop herself from searching out Zach, she was disappointed to find both the beach and the water devoid of any surfers.

Shifting the pies carefully in her hands, she craned her neck, but it was no use. He was gone.

Just as well. Her nerves couldn't take another encounter with him so soon, especially when she had no idea what to say to him.

*Sorry I tried to jump your bones last night. It's just that I'm tired of being a virgin, you see, tired of wondering, hoping, dreaming.*

So intent was she on her thoughts—and keeping one eye peeled on the shoreline—that she didn't hear the footsteps behind her until it was too late.

"Hannah."

With a startled gasp, she whirled quickly. She couldn't help it—the deep and unbearably familiar voice unsettled both her pulse, and then unfortunately, her balance.

Pies sailed high in the air.

Hannah had time to let out a scream of frustration before they came back down...directly on her. With a sharply indrawn breath—they were *ice*-cold!—she lifted her head, and glared at Zach.

Strawberries dripped off her chin, her shoulders, her chest. The gooey sauce ran down her dress, sticking to her skin, which was now clammy. Crust crumpled and hit the ground, along with the two tins that had been holding the pies together.

"What a mess!" Dropping to her knees, she stared in dismay at the disaster.

Zach set down his surfboard, then hit his knees too. "Let me help."

"You've done enough!"

He gathered the tins. Then he sat back on his heels and looked at her seriously. "I'm sorry." But his mouth curved suspiciously.

"Yeah, you look real sorry." Actually he looked...as mouthwateringly good as the strawberry pies smelled. He was still wet from the ocean, his wide shoulders and smooth, sleek chest gleamed. His exhaustion seemed to have vanished, his eyes sparkled with life, and his mouth... Lord, that mouth. It was curved softly, reminding her of all she wanted.

*It's all in the body language,* Tara had said.

So she gave that a shot, softening her expression, leaning in a little, giving him the best come-hither look she could manage.

"I *am* sorry," he said in a voice suddenly hushed with...with that *thing* that existed between them. His smile scrambled her brain. "Hannah, you're looking at me in that way, that way that makes me lose my train of thought. Stop it."

"I can't. Maybe *you'd* better stop looking at me."

"I can't. Let me..." And he leaned close, close enough that she could see his eyes darken, close enough to smell the outdoorsy, oceany, male scent of him.

Their knees touched, and Hannah thought she shouldn't feel weak just being in such close confines with him.

But then he did something that made her far weaker. "I have to taste you," he whispered. "Have to." He dipped his head and dragged his hot, open mouth over her bare shoulder, lapping at some of the strawberry goo there.

"Oh, my," she heard herself whisper as her

body reacted by trembling. It *was* in the body language! Hallelujah! She'd gotten it right!

He did it again, took another little nip, working his way across her collarbone to her other shoulder, before backtracking, lingering at the base of her throat, and Hannah could have sworn her eyes crossed with lust.

If he kept it up, she would dissolve into a little puddle of longing at his feet. "Zach—"

"Tell me this is stupid."

"This is stupid. Don't you dare stop."

A laugh escaped him, one that sounded more like a groan. His mouth took hers then, swallowing whatever she might have found the energy to say, but it was no longer important, nothing was except for their connection. It wasn't a demanding kiss, but slow and deep and leisurely, which was even more arousing.

The tins clattered to the ground as he slid his hands around her.

In response, she looped her arms around his neck, bringing their bodies flush to each other. She stuck to him immediately, the strawberry sauce acting like adhesive between her dress and his bare torso, and when he settled himself in the notch at the top of her thighs, she rocked to him, eliciting a deep-throated groan that vibrated from his chest to hers.

He rocked back, harder now, and she nearly wept at the need coursing through her. She lost herself in his taste and feel, just absolutely, completely lost herself. Lean, hard muscles shifted beneath her hands as she streaked them over his taut back, his shoulders, anything she could reach.

And from far, far away came the sound of heels on the path, then a very satisfied laugh.

*Tara.*

"I knew it," she chortled with glee, clapping her hands together. "I just knew it."

# 8

TARA STOOD THERE, smiling, noting Zach's hands on her best friend with a raised brow, but she said nothing. Her grin pretty much said it all.

She reached out and swiped at a particularly large chunk of pie still on Hannah's shoulder, then stuck that finger in her mouth and sucked. "Mmm, heavenly. Too bad it never made it to dinner."

Zach removed his hands from Hannah with shocking difficulty, though his heart and mind were racing. What had happened to keeping his damn distance? Instead Hannah was plastered to him from chest to thigh.

"Cat got your tongues, huh?" Tara asked sympathetically. "Don't worry, I understand. A kiss like that will make mush of anyone's brain." She winked at Hannah. "Next time come to me first. Apparently I've got the right stuff."

And with that, she walked away, humming cheerfully.

"What does that mean?" he asked Hannah.

Hannah tipped her head back and stared at the sky as if waiting for divine intervention.

"Don't tell me...you asked her for advice, too."

"She offered."

"Why didn't you just ask me?"

She stopped studying the sky and looked at him. "I thought I could do it without asking. I should have known better." She let out a tight laugh. "I tried damn near everything to make sure you knew what I wanted. I even offered you a condom with your coffee!"

A big drop of strawberry pie ran down her neck and dripped to her collarbone. It hovered there for a long second, quivering with motion, then hit the curve of her breast, just barely revealed by her sundress, before it disappeared behind the material.

Zach felt the stirring of the strange heat she always seemed to generate and tried to ignore the tightening of his body.

Impossible.

"You probably think I'm crazy," she said. "The way I went after you last night."

Her genuine misery cut right through him, and any distance he might have managed became impossible. "I didn't realize what you were doing then," he said. Though he should have when he thought about it, should have questioned why she hadn't told him they were booked, why she'd crawled into bed with him. "I'm sorry."

A grimace crossed her face. "Great. You didn't realize. And you can wonder why I needed tips?"

He didn't know what to do about her. She was getting to him, entering the never-before-penetrated zone around his heart, and he didn't want her there. "I don't care that you didn't know what you were doing."

"You...don't?"

"No." In fact, he couldn't get that little tidbit out of his head. In his wildest imagination he never would have thought her being inexperienced could be such a turn-on. "I guess what I care about is that you decided to...gain experience, and I just happened along. Any guy would have done."

"Oh, Zach." Her hand reached out, touched his chest. Electrified him. "No. That's not true."

"What if I hadn't shown up?"

She shoved back her hair and made a face when her fingers came in contact with a strawberry. "I don't know," she admitted.

Her honesty was nice, but frustrating. "That's just one of the reasons why we can't, Hannah."

"And the others?"

"Because..." Why? He suddenly couldn't remember. "Because you're Alexi's friend!"

"And here I thought you were such a wild rebel." Disdain crossed her face. "A true wild rebel wouldn't care about that."

"Okay then, how about because I've known you forever."

"That's silly. We're grown-ups now."

"We can't because..." His brain raced desperately. "Because I'm only here a few more days and you deserve more than that."

That irritated her. "I can decide what I deserve, thank you very much. For your information, I'm not looking for a relationship."

God help him. "That's supposed to make it okay? That you're just looking for sex?" he asked incredulously. No doubt, he was insane. This beautiful, intelligent, wonderful woman wanted him for sex only, and he was actually trying to talk her out of it. He should have his head examined.

"You don't want me." She looked devastated. "That's it. It's okay, I understand."

"I don't think you do."

"No, really."

"I want you." His voice was thick with that wanting. "But this is wrong."

"How can it be wrong? When I'm with you, I feel different. Good."

Well, great. Terrific. She felt good, and obviously he'd been the one to make her feel that way, which was great for the ego, but he was still confused as hell. And he had absolutely no idea how to proceed.

There was no denying certain life facts.

One, he still had time off.

Two, his side hurt only a little.

Three, he had Hannah watching him with the expression that made him want her more than he could remember ever wanting a woman, which reminded him that there was another night just in front of them, and then several more after that. "I feel good, too," he admitted. "With you."

The hope that statement put in her eyes was bad. Very bad. It meant that *he* was going to have to be the grown-up here. "Look, maybe I should go with my first instincts," he said. "The lodge is still booked. I'm sure there's other inns nearby, one that I can stay in—"

"No!" She reached out for him, touching his arms, brushing her body against his. Which meant she also brushed strawberry pie against him. He tried to mind, but didn't. "Don't leave. I don't want to feel as though I chased you away just because I—"

"Want my body?"

When he smiled, she laughed a little. "Yeah. Well, I'm a mess." Her smile seemed weak now. "I should clean up."

And he should offer to help. She wanted him to. But he didn't trust her not to try to seduce him again, and he didn't trust himself enough to resist her efforts.

"Well..." Her smile faded slowly. "See you later."

Another drop of strawberry slid down her collarbone, disappearing into the bodice of her dress with the rest. He watched it go, his mouth dry. His fingers itched, and at his sides, he fisted them. "Yeah. See you."

MUCH LATER THAT NIGHT, Zach climbed the stairs of the lodge. He waved at the Schwartzes, but kept moving, not giving them a chance to question how he'd fared with the "babes."

With a great deal of trepidation, he knocked at Hannah's door.

He would have given anything to avoid this, but he couldn't. He needed his duffel bag.

Hannah opened the door. She'd been sleeping,

he could see that now, and he made a sound of remorse that she waved away. "No, it's okay. I'm...glad you're here." Her voice was husky. She wore another T-shirt. It fell off one creamy shoulder and his mouth actually watered.

With the light behind her, she was perfectly silhouetted. Beneath the soft, worn material of her shirt he could see the outline of her lush breasts, the darker tips of her nipples. As he watched, they tightened, puckered, pressing against the cotton as if begging for attention.

Swallowing his groan, he met her gaze. "I just needed some clothes."

"For the couch in the office."

"Yes."

"Oh, Zach, stay here."

"I can't." At just the thought, his body surged to attention.

"My couch is far more comfortable. Really," she said.

"I don't want the couch. I want you. And I don't *want* to want you." To torture himself, he came closer, leaning in to softly kiss her. "Good night, Hannah."

With one last longing glimpse of what he couldn't have, all those long limbs and sweet, warm body, he brushed another kiss along her temple.

Oh yeah, *there* was the way to maintain his distance. "Sleep tight," he whispered and grabbed his bag.

"Zach... This is silly. Stay. I promise to behave."

He looked at her, all warm and cozy and flushed. With all he had, he wanted to stay too, wanted to bury himself deep in her warm, giving body, wanted to love her until...

And wasn't that the kicker? The true problem? He could imagine himself loving her, not just for one night, but forever.

He couldn't.

She wouldn't.

"Stay."

She could have no idea how much he wanted to do that. Or maybe she did. Maybe she felt the same and was too afraid to admit it, as was he. Two lost, lonely, uncertain souls.

God, he was so tired. It was all catching up to him, resulting in an exhaustion he couldn't seem to shake. "Why, Hannah? Why should I stay?"

She seemed startled. "Because I think you'll be more comfortable—"

"Truth."

"Okay, because I want you near me." Her voice lowered to a whisper as she repeated it. "I want you near me."

Damn. He couldn't resist that. He wanted to be near her too.

He made his way to the couch, waited while she went back to bed and shut her bedroom door.

He wished it had a lock on it. With a hard-on to end all hard-ons, he lay down and stared at the ceiling, willing sleep to come.

It took a long time.

MUCH LATER Zach came suddenly awake.

In the dark room, Hannah stood there, watching him. He stretched and rolled over to look at the clock. Three in the morning.

"Couldn't sleep," she said, holding something behind her back.

Oh, boy. She had those huge, expressive eyes and wild hair, looking vulnerable and a whole lot sexy, and she was going to try to seduce him again, he could feel it. He was certain she had absolutely no idea how her fumbling, bumbling attempts were doing exactly that.

"Candles in here would be a bad idea," he said quickly. "The desk over there is so loaded with stuff, you'll start a fire."

"I don't have candles."

"And music will wake up the guests."

"No music, either, not this time." She smiled.

His heart tipped right on its side. Dammit. "Luckily enough it's so dark in here, dark enough I can't see anything. So..." Just thinking the words had him hard. "Flashing skin won't work, either."

"I know."

Something new then. Terrific. It wouldn't take much. And he was so exhausted he knew if he didn't get her out of here, *now*, his own control wasn't going to hold.

From behind her back, she pulled out a book. "I thought maybe this would help."

*How To Seduce A Man And Keep Him Seduced.*

His body jerked. "Hannah—"

"Yeah. It was stupid."

Dammit, she sounded defeated. So certain no man could ever find her attractive. "Hannah...it's not what you think."

"I know, I just thought I'd try one last time."

"I told you why we couldn't," he said desperately.

"Yes," she repeated dutifully. "You're my best friend's brother. You're my brother's best friend. Oh, and you're leaving in a few days."

"Yes." Not daring to touch her, he willed her to understand.

"And while with another woman you'd most definitely go for a quickie affair," she added. "You won't with me because I'm not the type to inspire such passion."

"I never said that."

"You didn't have to."

Forget not touching her. He grabbed her hand, and nearly shoved it down the front of his sweat bottoms to show her exactly what kind of passion she evoked in him.

But that would be a bad idea, *very* bad.

Instead, he tugged her down on the couch beside him, a mistake he realized instantly because she wasn't wearing anything beneath her T-shirt, so that all those warm, soft curves snuggling up to him made him want to wrap himself around her and never let go.

*Never.*

Dammit.

She shifted, levering herself up with her arms to look at him. "Zach—" Her legs slid over his so that she was straddling him. In that position, that innocent but oh-so-erotic position, she suddenly went utterly still.

"Oh, my," she whispered. "You're..."

"Aroused?" He gave her a tight smile. "I've been in this sorry state for two nights now, thank you very much. Can you see how wrong you are now? It isn't you, surely you can feel that much."

She licked her dry lips. "But I don't get it. This should be so simple. I *know* your life down in L.A. is important to you. I *know* you crave wild adventure and excitement, you've *always* craved that. And I *know* Avila doesn't do it for you. I'm not expecting anything other than this, Zach. I'm not."

"You should." Unable to help himself, he slid his hands up her smooth thighs, around to her bottom, beneath her T-shirt. He filled his hands with her.

"I'm not going to beg you," she whispered.

In a second, *he'd* be the one begging. He couldn't stop his fingers from roaming, from skimming over as much of her as he could.

"Zach...."

"No," he whispered, forcing his fingers still, though it was the hardest thing he'd ever done.

She let out a rough sound of wanting, but she rose with grace and dignity, took her book and left him alone.

Sleep was impossible.

THE NEXT AFTERNOON, Hannah ran across the bluffs to the stairs, then down to the beach. The sand sank between her toes as she walked to the water's edge.

She swam like clockwork every day—except when beautiful men named Zach Thomas came to town and messed up her thought process—which was why she could tear off her clothes and have her bathing suit already beneath.

Today she had the beach to herself. And though she loved their guests, loved talking to them, for once she was grateful for the solitude.

The water was icy, and did exactly what she'd banked on—cleared her brain in one quick wave that sucked the air right out of her.

She held her breath and dove into the next wave, gliding beneath the water she knew better than the back of her own hand.

Here she was at home. Alone. No demands on her time, no one needing her.

It went without saying that she needed no one in return.

There was a storm brewing, and the water was choppy, but she could handle it. She *needed* to handle it. She swam straight out.

From shore, someone called her name.

Zach.

He was standing, some twenty-five yards back now, watching her with grim worry.

"I'm fine," she shouted.

"Too far," she thought she heard him call. He glanced up at the churning sky.

"I'm fine," she said again, but he ripped off his shirt, toed off his shoes and dove in after her. Hannah sighed in annoyance, but there was something else there, too, something far too close to a thrill.

*He* was coming after *her*. She glanced at the sky and decided maybe he was right, there was a storm moving in. Just as she turned back, Zach called her name.

She couldn't help it, laughter bubbled, and enjoying that he'd come for her, she pumped her arms and legs faster, heading toward him now.

That's when it hit, a cramp that shot up her entire right leg and nearly paralyzed her with shocking pain. She couldn't believe how much it hurt—it was everything she could do just to breathe.

A swell towered over her head, but she couldn't duck it, couldn't body surf it, couldn't do anything but double over with agony.

The wave hit full force, dragging her under.

When she managed to surface, Zach was right there in front of her, his face filled with terror.

She had time to think he must be a fantastic swimmer to have covered that distance in a fraction of the time it had taken her, before she went under again. Then Zach had her.

"What is it?" he demanded as he reached for her. "What's wrong?"

"Cramp." She gasped, struggling to take in only air and not the entire ocean.

The wind had picked up, and so had the size and the frequency of the waves. She squirmed to try to alleviate the pain, and went under again.

"I've got you." Zach's arms slipped around her, and they were firm and filled with welcoming strength.

The storm hit with a vengeance, sending a harsh, driving rain in their faces in tune with the choppy swells.

"Hold on to me!" he yelled, as he started toward shore.

But she couldn't hold on, couldn't do anything but convulse with pain. Another swell hit them. They both went under then, but he had her, had her tight to him, and she knew he wouldn't let go. The pain was incredible, but it blocked out the heavy current, the stinging rain, everything but the shore wavering in and out in front of her.

Zach never hesitated, just swam with long, sure, powerful strokes, though she could feel the tension radiating from every bone in his body.

Another huge swell hit them, and Hannah was certain she'd be ripped away from Zach, but he held tight, refusing to let her go.

"Almost there," he said breathlessly.

Hannah was lost in her world of agony. When she finally felt the sand beneath her feet, she nearly burst into tears, *would* have burst into tears, but she couldn't breathe for the pain.

They dropped heavily to the wet sand, gasping for air.

Zach leaned over her, holding her still. As it continued to rain down on them, he pushed his fingers hard into her cramping muscles, so hard she saw stars, but finally, long moments later, bit by bit, she was able to relax. "Better," she managed.

Completely spent, he collapsed next to her. His arms came around her hard. Together they lay there beneath the rain and wind, shivering, but without the energy to move.

"Well, that was a nice swim," he was finally able to say.

Hannah was busy concentrating on the heat of his chest, the very lovely sound of his heartbeat beneath her ear, his arms snug and secure around her. "I'm glad you were there."

"Me, too." He rubbed his cheek over her hair, but still neither of them moved.

"Thank you," she said quietly. "Without you—"

"Don't. I don't even want to think about it."

A few moments went by while they concentrated on being alive. "Zach?" she asked after awhile.

"Yeah?"

"This didn't have anything to do with...you know."

"Seducing me?"

"Yeah."

"I know." He smiled. "Saving you didn't have anything to do with me continuing to try to resist you."

She managed a rusty laugh. "Okay. As long as we're straight."

The wind whipped over them and she shivered. Zach let out a low sound of remorse. "A shower," he decided, surging to his feet. "*Hot* water."

She couldn't help imagining them in her

shower, together, all slick, sleek, hot, drenched, soapy skin…

"Hannah." His voice was ragged. "Stop those thoughts."

"Okay." But she slid her chest against his, just to get closer to his warmth.

His gaze dipped down to her bathing suit.

She was chilled through to the bone.

They both stared at her hard nipples, pressing against the material. He groaned softly and closed his eyes. "Shower," he said again. "Hot one for you, cold one for me."

# 9

ZACH GOT HIS OWN ROOM the next day. It should have taken his mind off his troubles, but his mind was occupied with the image of Hannah sprawled across the sand the day before, water beaded across her body, her eyes filled with hunger.

She'd still wanted him. He'd wanted her.

Even with the storm, she'd been hot and bothered, and so had he.

He still was.

And yet, whether she wanted to realize it or not, she wasn't the quickie affair type, and he was discovering that neither was he.

It was all so complicated, and complicated, in Zach's opinion, was to be avoided, at all costs. Especially here. But his heart didn't seem to be in agreement with his brain.

Which was the only reason he didn't just leave. He could go back to Los Angeles early, could certainly prepare to return to work, to his life, but he couldn't seem to do it. He could tell himself he wasn't quite ready for the physical demands of being a cop, that he wasn't all better, but that was a big, fat lie.

It was Hannah, the first woman in far too long to stir his passion, his heart and soul.

She reminded him there was far more to life than burying who he was to do his job.

Hannah walked him to his new room, though he could have easily found it himself. He could have also done without that smirk in the Schwartzes' eyes as they passed the upper sitting area.

But he had bigger worries. Hannah had that stubborn look in her eyes, the look that said maybe she wasn't finished with him yet.

Only he couldn't resist another sweet, unbearably erotic attempt, he just couldn't. At least she was dressed modestly, in a blouse and slacks, with not a candle or condom in sight.

They stepped inside his room. Zach dropped his bag and realized he could hardly hold his head up.

"Sleep," she whispered, gently pushing him toward the bedroom. She must have had mercy on him because she stayed by the door. "I'll let myself out."

His body warred with his mind, wanting to

take her with him to the bed, but thankfully his mind won out.

He was asleep before he could even cover himself up.

THE MOST WONDERFUL and strangest dream came to him.

Hannah's hands were moving over his bare chest, followed by her mouth, and he was unable to hold back his own frenzied reaction. He didn't want it to end, this amazing dream.

She touched him again, dropping hot, open-mouthed kisses down his belly, that left him panting. Too long, it'd been too long for him. No one should have to be so strong as to resist this.

If she so much as touched him one more time it would be over, and he tried to tell her so, tried to hold her back, but she wouldn't allow it. Sliding him onto his back, she followed him down, down, entwining their legs, rubbing her cotton-clad torso over his until he could do nothing but moan her name.

It was heaven, absolute heaven.

And it was a dream.

*Wasn't it?*

He'd thought so, but his heart was pounding, hands gripping soft skin—*real* skin—his body tight as an arrow. Hannah was over him, her long hair teasing his chest, her hips in his fists, her legs spread to accommodate his.

Reaching up, she pulled off her shirt, baring her breasts to him before he could draw another breath. Pale curves shimmered in the moonlight, tight, dusky peaks beckoning him. Then she shimmied out of the rest of her clothes.

"Hannah, wait..." She was perfect, beyond perfect. And he was already so aroused his toes were tingling, his body just one touch away from exploding. "We're dreaming. *I'm* dreaming—"

She took his hands and slid them up over her flat belly, past her ribs, letting out a hum of pleasure as his fingers took over and cupped her breasts in his palms. "Not dreaming," she whispered fiercely. She lifted up on her knees so that his erection nestled at her hot, wet center, poised for entry.

He was gasping for breath as if he'd just run a marathon, every inch of him dying, *dying* for her. "*Wait*," he pleaded into her hair, sucking in a harsh breath when she shifted her hips, taking the very tip of him inside her. He gripped her hips and with his last ounce of control, held her still.

*Stop,* his mind commanded. *Set her away from you.*

"I don't have any...protection," his body said instead.

"You...don't?"

She sounded so frustrated he let out a low laugh. "No, I— No."

"I do." Her eyes were so dark and round he could have drowned in them. "Alexi gave me a box of condoms last Christmas. It was supposed to be a joke because I never need them..."

God bless Alexi, was Zach's only rational thought as Hannah held up a foil packet. Then her hands were on him, inexpertly but oh-so-deliciously touching him, and because he was so close, so very close, he pushed her fingers aside and finished the job himself.

Then finally, finally, he pulled her down for a long, deep, wet kiss, completely forgetting why this was a bad idea. Forgetting why he'd ever thought he could walk away from Avila without having her. He rolled her beneath him, ran his hands over her and thrust inside her body.

He didn't get far.

Lifting his head, he stared down into her glazed eyes. Her face was flushed with pleasure, her eyes alight with glowing need. She was biting her full lower lip, and she looked so incredibly turned on, he could barely speak.

"Please," she whispered, arching, thrusting up, running her hands over him. "Oh, please."

As if he could resist. Everything had become a haze of desire and need and friction. She gripped his hips as he cupped her face. Together they surged, and together they broke through the wall of her resistance.

*Wall of resistance.*

If he'd still been groggy, even partly asleep, he came suddenly, sharply, shockingly fully awake in that moment, and froze.

*Definitely not a dream.* He looked down into her face, saw the truth in her shining eyes. Groaning her name, he dropped his forehead to hers. "Oh, Hannah..."

"Please," she said again.

Tenderness, and a whole host of other things he didn't want to think about, flooded him. "Are you okay?"

Her hips were thrusting helplessly toward his, assuring him she was fine and needing more. "Zach...I need..."

"Yes," he whispered, dipping down to kiss her, to streak off her few tears with his thumbs. "I know. I know what you need." And to make sure she got it, he ran his hands over her, her breasts, her belly, everywhere, rearing up so he could slip a hand between her thighs, using his fingers to pay special homage to her very center, which was hot and slippery.

She cried out and he urged her on, whispering erotic promises, coaxing, teasing, keeping up the motion of his fingers while she began to shudder. Her contractions triggered his own undeniable explosion, and together they took that sweet, wild plunge into ecstasy.

THE NEXT THING Hannah knew, she was blinking at the ceiling in orgasmic shock, having just had the most amazing experience of her very inexperienced life.

She'd done it.

*It.*

And it had been every bit as good as she'd dared to hope. *Better.*

Her earlier exhaustion was gone, completely vanished into the same thin air her innocence had gone. Wide-eyed, she lay there on her back, still half covered by a large, warm, very cozy male body, and she felt great.

Zach's breathing had evened out now, becoming deep and steady. It hadn't been so just moments ago; he'd been breathing as erratically as she, and just the memory of that, the power of knowing she'd caused it, sent a delicious little aftershock through her.

But now he was asleep, his body possessively claiming hers even in dreamland. And it was that supposedly awkward and dreaded *afterwards* that Tara and Alexi always joked about. Well, she was determined not to suffer through it. Nothing was going to ruin the euphoria she felt.

Not even knowing that what she and Zach had shared was more than just a romantic interlude. When she hadn't been looking, her heart had jumped into the fray. Now it was still there, beating like a drum with joy.

Unable to resist, she stroked a hand down his long, sleek back. In his sleep, he arched toward her touch, making a deep, indistinct, very male sound.

Soon everyone would be up. She didn't want to share her magical night. In fact, she'd rather clean toilets for an entire year than admit what she and Zach had done, not because she was ashamed in any way, but because it had been so...well, amazing.

Earth-shattering.

And wasn't that just the problem? This was to

have been just a simple thing, only there was nothing simple about it.

She'd actually learned something about herself, something she'd never expected—despite being basically man-shy, she *could* be warm and affectionate. Sensual. Even wild with passion.

She really could give a part of herself.

She'd always wondered. And in that wondering, had always held a part of herself back. Maybe it'd been self-preservation, she didn't know.

But she hadn't held back last night. And now she was facing the implications of that—that no matter what she'd promised Zach, her feelings for him weren't casual, and sure as hell weren't temporary. One night hadn't been enough.

And while she knew she could have more nights, a few anyway, she was deathly afraid that wouldn't be enough either.

And yet for Zach they would be.

What a mess.

But it was *her* mess, and she wouldn't drag him any further into it, nor would she ruin what was left of his time off.

Gently, so as not to awaken him, she tried to lift the arm he'd slung across her belly. It weighed a ton. Very quietly she wriggled, trying to scoot out from beneath him. She'd nearly gotten free when his arm suddenly tightened.

He opened one eye.

"Hi," she said inanely. "I didn't mean to wake you—"

"I've heard that one before." His voice was deep, husky.

And thrilling.

So was the way he lifted his arm to trace a finger over her jaw, tucking a strand of hair behind her ear.

"I was just going to slip out of here—"

"No." He tugged her close again in a nice hug that made her want to melt.

"You need your rest," she insisted. "But I don't, I'm not tired—"

The way he was looking at her made her want to hold him forever. She had to get out before she gave herself away. "So I'll just—"

"Hannah."

"I forgot to water the fern on the landing, and I think that—"

"Hannah." With a sigh, he opened his other eye. *"Sleep."*

"But—"

"Shh." Gently, he set a finger to her lips then managed to lift his head and look at her. "I know we need to talk, but I swear I can't put together a single, rational thought. Can we sleep first, just for a little while? Please?"

His eyes were dark and serious. His arms were strong around her, making her feel warm and safe in a way she hadn't felt in a long time, if ever. He wasn't trying to avoid her, or put her off, he was just plain exhausted.

And she was falling for him, big time. If he found out, or even got a hint of it, he'd regret their night together, and she refused to let that happen.

"*You* sleep," she said quietly, lifting her hand to touch his face just because she wanted to feel him one more time. "I'll just—"

He nuzzled his face against her neck. "You'll sleep too," he said, holding her tight. "Talk later."

"Zach."

"*Sleep.*"

She'd never been one to follow directions or take authority well, but she didn't feel bossed around. The opposite actually.

She felt…cared for. And so she did what he said.

She slept.

# 10

ZACH WOKE UP ALONE, and refused to admit he wished Hannah hadn't left, that he'd had her all night long and it still hadn't been enough.

With all his restless energy, he ended up at the beach, where he surfed his troubles away. When he was done, refreshingly numb so that hopefully he couldn't think, he took the path through the grounds of the lodge.

There was a couple on a bench there, wrapped in each other's arms and kissing as if their lives depended on it.

Newlyweds, he figured, with an odd mix of envy and disgust.

Was he going to ever be that much in love? Scary thought. One he immediately dismissed.

He concentrated on his surroundings. He was amazed by all the color and beauty. Someone, probably a group of someones, worked damn hard here. It was a wonderful haven, with the wind blowing lightly, the sound of the surf providing mother nature's music.

The gardens couldn't be the doing of Alexi—she had what his family had always called a "black thumb," killing even the most hardy of houseplants when they'd been young.

And somehow he couldn't imagine the elegant and sophisticated Tara getting dirt beneath her carefully manicured nails and sullying her clothes.

Definitely not her style.

"That's the way," came a sweet, coaxing female voice from the other side of a bush.

Zach stopped in surprise. He recognized that voice.

"That's the way I like to see it."

He'd have known it was Hannah even if her voice hadn't registered right away because his pulse all but stopped, then sped up like a locomotive.

"Come on baby, there you go."

Zach rounded the corner, not sure what he expected to find, but tense and battle-ready—which if he'd stopped to think about, would have made him laugh.

He had no claim on her.

But the sight before him was an even bigger surprise than her words.

She was on her hands and knees, her face

streaked down one side, her hands covered to her wrists in soil.

She was talking to the daisies.

Startled at his abrupt appearance, Hannah sat back on her heels and blinked at him before smiling self-consciously. "Hello."

"Do you always talk to the plants?"

"My plants like to be talked to."

"You did all this?"

She seemed startled by the question, and she relaxed, making him realize she'd been tense enough to shatter.

Because of him? Undoubtedly.

*Distance,* he reminded himself. She'd managed to find it, he needed to do the same.

"I love to grow things," she said.

"It's beautiful out here." *And so are you.*

"Thank you." She rose gracefully to her feet, her long, bare legs as streaked with dirt as the rest of her.

He stared at them so long he nearly didn't realize she was walking away from him. "Wait!"

When she did, he was at a loss as to what to say. "Last night...that was beautiful, too."

"Oh, Zach..." Something vulnerable and haunting crossed her features.

"Is it that awful?" he asked quietly. "The remembering?"

"The opposite." A wry smile crossed her face. "It's just that I thought it best if...well." Drawing a deep breath, she sent him a sad smile. "Be safe, Zach."

"Are you saying goodbye then?"

Her silence was his answer, and he felt his own spear of hurt. "I should tell you, I can't seem to walk away."

"Me, either," she whispered. "I just don't know what to say. You...just standing there, you make my knees weak. I'm feeling so out of my element."

"Just about everything you've done since I saw you again has made my knees weak. And if it helps, I'm also way out of my element." Because he had to, he pulled her close.

She gasped and tried to pull away. "I'll get you filthy!"

"Dirt, strawberry pie, it's all the same to me." He streaked his hands down her back, and at the connection she stopped fighting him and slid her arms around his neck.

"This is a very bad idea," she said, even as she hugged him tighter.

"Definitely." Burying his face in her hair, he

held her close, and all the feelings he'd been fighting struggled to the surface.

Heat. Hunger. Desire.

Yearning.

Her fingers wound themselves in his hair, and she let out a long sigh. "Somehow when you're not right in front of me I can tell myself I'm imagining all this...this *stuff* I feel right now."

"Me, too."

"What are we doing, Zach?"

"I haven't a clue. I just know I feel so alive when I'm with you."

She lifted her head and looked at him.

"I like it," he whispered. "Feeling alive. And I think I make you feel the same way."

"You do, but you're going away. I have to remember that."

"Yes, we both know how it's going to end. We always did."

"And that's supposed to make it easy?" She closed her eyes. "I'm sorry. After all, I'm the one that started this."

"So let's finish it." The words shocked him as much as her. "We have a few days left."

"I can't, I can't let my heart get in this."

He had the terrifying feeling it was too late for both of them.

"It all happened so quickly. I didn't expect that. It's going to be so hard to let you go."

"Then don't think about it," he suggested. "Think about last night, and how good it was. How good it could be right now if we run up to my room."

"Don't." She let out a low, nervous laugh. "Don't even talk! You could coax me into doing anything with that voice of yours."

"Really?" That had interesting—and erotic—possibilities.

Her gaze met his and held. "Really." Another rueful laugh escaped her. "Please...don't even try." Her voice quivered, and her hands, which she tucked under her arms, shook.

"Hannah..." But what could he say? That he'd never hurt her? But he would, just by being what he was, who he was.

And since it was too late, they were both bound for anguish no matter what happened now, he didn't want to let her go. "There are telephones in Los Angeles, you know. And e-mail." God, he'd really lost his mind now. "The drive isn't so bad really—"

"You're only saying that now, in the heat of the moment, but you don't mean it." She shook her head, her eyes huge and solemn. "Don't make me a promise you can't keep, Zach."

He cupped her face and traced her mouth with his thumb, unsure of everything except how he felt when she was in his arms.

"Don't," she repeated, but she tipped her head up for a kiss, which he gave her. It was a heart and soul kiss, and they both sighed, deepening it until they tore apart, breathless. Staring at each other.

Then she walked away, leaving him alone in the garden, lonely heart pounding in tune to the waves.

ZACH SPENT THAT NIGHT ALONE. It was nothing new, he spent most nights alone, and yet he'd never felt so lonely in his life.

By morning, he decided physical exercise was what he needed to shake the melancholy. Two miles later and two nearly collapsed lungs, he sank gratefully to the beach in front of the lodge.

"Some relaxing vacation," Alexi noted dryly, coming up behind him to sit next to him. She handed him a towel and a bottle of water and sent him a little smile.

In the way of family, she didn't bother him with trivial details or minor observations. No, not his sister, who knew him better than most. Instead she waited until he caught his breath, until he tipped the water bottle to his mouth.

Then she went directly for the kill. "You going to sleep with Hannah?"

He nearly drowned himself.

She waited patiently while he recovered.

He glared at her.

"Are you going to hurt my best friend?" she asked calmly.

"What makes you think it's *Hannah* who's going to get hurt?"

"Please. *Your* heart is safe, it always has been safe. How can it be anything else when you put work first? I'm not worried about you." But then she relented. "Should I be?"

"Nah. I'm tough."

"Oh yeah. You're rough and tough, you're the big, bad, older brother who's invincible, right?" She sighed and smacked him upside the back of his head. "Get a grip, Zach. Matters of the heart can lay even a superhero low."

"Who said anything about matters of the heart?"

"I did, because in case you didn't notice, that's what this is."

Zach stared grimly out at the waves. "She's just looking for something new and exciting."

"You don't really believe that."

No, he didn't. But believing that it was *him* Hannah wanted was just as unsettling.

"So? What are you going to do?"

"Alexi...don't."

"Don't what? Don't tell the truth? That for years Tara and have I have watched Hannah put everyone else's needs before her own? First her family, then us. She always covers for us, whenever we need it, no matter what, and much as it shames me to admit it, it never occurred to us that we were taking advantage of her. She'd do anything for the people she cares about, and it's time we do something for her back. So she wants to see what she's missing. What's wrong with that? Especially when she's missing plenty!"

Not anymore, he thought, digging his heels into the sand. Thanks to him and his very questionable self-control, Hannah wasn't missing anything now.

"Do you really want her to find out exactly what with some guy that won't care about her as much as you do?"

He stared at the waves and tried to tell himself

it was okay that Hannah would eventually find a man to love her the way she deserved.

"Do it, Zach. Sleep with her and make it right. Show her everything she wants to know."

He'd already shown her, and he wanted to do it again. "And then what?" he asked. "Just leave? Don't you think that will make it worse?"

"No," she said. "I don't. Because this time you'll come back."

He stared at her, saw her thoughts as if she'd spoken them out loud. "I'm not going to fall in love, Alexi. Not a chance."

"Hmmm."

"I'm not."

She smiled. "Methinks maybe you protest too much."

Dammit. "I love you, I really do, but I'm not ever coming back for good."

Alexi's smile faded. "I know."

Zach tipped up his head and watched a lazy white cloud make its way across the sky. "Besides, we both know I have nothing to offer a woman permanently."

"Oh, my God."

"What?"

"You just said *woman* and *permanent* in the

same sentence." She softened immediately. "Oh, Zach."

"No." He managed a laugh and sat up straighter. "Don't use that dreamy voice on me." She merely smiled and he lifted up a hand. "I mean it, Alexi. Wipe that look off your face."

"There's hope."

"No."

"Yes. You're already half in love, you're just not ready to admit it."

His heart nearly stopped. "Stop it."

"Can't." Smiling into the sun, she plopped back on the sand and tucked her hands beneath her head, looking satisfied with the world. "You and Hannah, it'd be just too perfect for words."

"No, it wouldn't."

"I'll miss her of course. So much. Just promise you'll stay for the rest of your time off, just to give us a little time together, you and me. Like old times. Please?"

How did she so effortlessly manipulate him into both guilt and remorse?

"Zach... Please?"

He didn't want to deny her, but to do as she asked and in such close proximity to Hannah... "You want me to stay even if the only thing that's going to happen between Hannah and me is a friendship?"

"A friendship?" Her expression told him how ridiculous she thought *that* was.

"We have a genuine affection and warmth for each other, but it's not going further than that. I'm going back to L.A. soon, and Hannah...she belongs here, no matter what's between us."

Alexi lifted a brow.

"Or not between us," he muttered.

"Are you saying you've *already* slept together?"

He clenched his jaw tight and remained silent.

"No, of course not." She laughed. "I would have known. Right? Zach?"

He just shook his head. "Stop it."

"Okay, tell me this. *Truthfully.* That warmth and affection you mentioned...could it have been more? You know, if things were different?"

Different as in if he wasn't a cop? Or if she didn't live so far from his work? Different as in if they both weren't afraid of facing their emotions? Would they be able to make a go of the wonderful and inexplicable feelings between them then?

"Yeah," he finally said. "It could have been more."

Much more.

"Maybe you could talk to her about it." Alexi nodded toward the bluffs, where Hannah had appeared.

Her hair whipped about in the light wind, and the sundress she wore danced around her long legs. She walked the path away from them. Just watching her go caused a deep ache. A need.

And only she could fill it. "We don't really have anything to talk about," he said.

"I'm betting you do." Alexi rose to leave, but she stopped to give him a kiss. "Love you, Zach."

Then he was alone, on the sand, with Hannah fifty feet away. As if she sensed him, she slowly turned, then looked right at him.

He walked toward her. "Hey."

"Hey." She sent him a small smile. "Alexi pestering you again?"

"As always. She's opinionated, especially about..."

"About...?"

"Us," he said bluntly. "She's fond of meddling."

"Does she know about the other night?"

"She's trying to figure it out."

"She just wants to know if she lost."

"Lost what?"

"Oh..." She bit her lower lip. "Some silly bet."

"About?"

"About...toilets."

"You guys had a bet about toilets?"

"It was nothing, really. You see, Tara and Alexi started this stupid bet on who could get *un*single for the summer."

"Unsingle."

"Yes. It seemed so easy—only it wasn't easy at all, not for me, because I never date. So I decided to make my own personal goal." She gave him a rueful look. "And I think you know what that was."

"This...was all about a bet?" Any warm and fuzzy feelings he'd been secretly harboring pretty much disintegrated on the spot. Never mind that he'd been worrying *she* would want more from *him,* when he couldn't give it. The idea that what they'd shared had been all because of a bet hurt more than he could have imagined. "So what did you win?"

"Zach, it only started out that way, I—"

"What did you win, Hannah?"

"Nothing, because I didn't tell them what... happened between us."

"What will you win when they find out?"

Remorse flashed across her features. "Well,

that's the thing. It's not so much a winning, it's what happens to the loser."

"And what would that be?"

"They have to clean the toilets—all of them in the lodge—for the entire summer."

"So I saved you a bottle of disinfectant and some elbow grease?" he asked in disbelief.

"I honestly figured I'd lose," she said earnestly. "But then you showed up—"

"And you decided the heck with cleaning toilets, I'll just sleep with Zach. He'll oblige me."

"No! No, it wasn't like that at all. When I saw you again, after all that time, it brought back feelings I'd had for you..." She hesitated, glanced at him to see how he was taking this, and clearly decided he wasn't taking it well at all, so she speeded up. "It was awful."

"Awful," he repeated dully.

"Yeah, but not in the way you think."

"Maybe you should explain."

"I'm not sure I can. It's just that I looked at you and something...*happened*." She blinked at him, as if willing him to understand. "I felt as though we were the same, both lonely and aching for something, but not knowing what. It was so good to see you again," she said simply. "It was like the homecoming I didn't know I was missing. I didn't know how to react."

"So you slept with me."

"Well, it wasn't easy," she said with a low laugh, but her smile disappeared when he didn't smile back.

"Okay, yes, so I slept with you." She sighed. "I was tired of being a virgin, okay? Tired of wondering what it would be like to be held and kissed and *wanted* by a man. By a man who maybe cared about me just a little."

"Well you got that last part right at least," he told her grudgingly. "I care about you, and more than just a little."

"Really?"

God, the look in her eyes hurt. "Really, but—"

"But we both agreed this was only temporary, from the very beginning. I know, I remember." She watched him very carefully. "Would you have wanted it to be...more?"

"No." But wasn't that the kicker? He was no longer sure about that.

# 11

"SO...DID YOU do the deed with Zach yet?"

The three of them, Hannah, Alexi and Tara, were in the kitchen for their nightly ritual—junk food.

Hannah stared at Alexi, thankful she'd already swallowed the last bite of her brownie, which was tonight's dessert of choice.

The three of them had been meeting like this since they'd opened the lodge. It was their favorite time of the day. Usually they discussed the comings and goings of the guests, or their employees, or even financial stuff, but mostly they just sat around and enjoyed each other and the peace and quiet.

"Well? Did you?"

"I don't really want to talk about it," Hannah said.

"Really?" Alexi looked at her, shocked at the thought that one of them would hold out on good gossip. "Why not?"

"Because..." Why not? "Because..."

"Because you're falling for him."

"Really? Let me see." Tara came close and inspected Hannah's face carefully. "Hmmm...not necessarily true," she said over her shoulder to Alexi. "It could just be the triple decker ice cream she consumed for lunch, coupled with the five brownies she just inhaled."

"You're saying that look is caused by *sugar* overload and not *male* overload?" Alexi asked.

The two of them stood there discussing her, staring into her face, as if she wasn't right there. Laughing, Hannah pushed them both away. "Go on, both of you. If you see anything in my eyes, it's annoyance. At you. Good night."

She escaped, then leaned weakly against the kitchen door, staring at the curved staircase that led to the rooms.

Was Zach up there?

She realized she was holding her breath, and she slowly let it out, knowing it shouldn't matter where he was.

If only that was the truth.

She forced herself to go directly to her room, where she wandered around until the knock came.

To her shock, it was Zach, and he looked every bit as baffled and uncertain as she was. It was a good look on him though, and just seeing him made her hurt.

When she just stared at him, he sent her one of his most irresistible grins. "The Schwartzes are watching, you know. Waiting to see how long it takes me to talk you into letting me in. You're killing my reputation."

"You can't come in," she told him. "I might do something embarrassing, like throw myself at you."

He sent her a tight smile. "I'm fairly certain I've alienated you enough today so that my virtue is safe."

Unable to hold back her own smile at that, she stepped back. "Come in then. At your own risk, of course."

"Of course." He moved past her, into the middle of the room, then turned back to face her. "I gave up my room."

"You...what?"

"The inn is overbooked. Tara was downstairs tearing out her hair."

"Oh, poor thing. I need to go help."

"You worked a double shift already. She's got it handled. But I gave up my room, and—" He sent her another one of his smiles, this one touchingly uncertain.

Her heart tugged, which really annoyed her.

"Is your couch still available?" he asked unexpectedly.

"Is my—" She narrowed her eyes and studied him. "No."

"No?"

"*No.*"

"Why not?"

"Because I'll probably forget myself and look into your eyes, which will make me melt, dammit, and then the next thing I know we'll be…*you know*, and quite frankly, Zach, my heart just can't take it."

"Maybe I want you to melt." He took a step toward her. "Maybe I've thought it all over and decided it doesn't matter to me what got us together the other night, that I'm just glad it happened." Another step, and her heart leaped. "Maybe I want it to happen again." He took the last step between them. "And again."

He was standing before her now, his face tense, his entire *body* tense. "Maybe I think that Los Angeles isn't *that* far away, that I think we should do whatever it takes to ride this thing through to the end."

She shook her head, suddenly, terribly, very

afraid. "You swallowed too much sea water when you were surfing today. That must be it."

"Okay, you don't believe me." He nodded his understanding. "Hell, I hardly believe it myself. I can give you all the time you need to mull it over."

"You have only a few days left."

"That's not necessarily true."

She looked at him, wary. "I don't know what you mean. I thought you didn't want to leave any loose ends."

The hurt in her voice was unmistakable, and his fault. "Hannah—"

"No, I already know everything there is to know. Your job, your lifestyle, your everything, doesn't leave room for any entanglements. Don't you see? *That's* what made it all okay for me, because I *knew*. At least at first, it was okay." She sighed. "But afterwards, the truth stared me in the face. I was only kidding myself. I...I felt something more than just lust, and it scares me to death."

He knew the feeling, all too well. "Hannah..."

"It can't happen again."

Yes, he'd thought that, too. But he felt empty just thinking about it.

Totally, completely, devastatingly empty.

"Maybe I need more than a few more days to recover from the shooting," he said softly.

Her eyes were wide, still wary. "But you love your job."

"Yeah. But the job could wait. If it had to."

"Don't do it. Don't you dare do something like that for me."

"How do you know it would be for you?"

"Wouldn't it?"

"Maybe it'd be for both of us."

"No." There was more than a little panic in her voice. "Because you *would* eventually go back, and it would be worse then, so much, much worse. So just stop it, stop looking at me like that, like you really, really care, okay?"

"Well, how about I don't look at you at all?" He touched her then, slid his hands up her arms, then back down until just their fingers were connected. Slowly he pulled her close in a hug devastatingly easy and warm. "There." He buried his face in the soft, vulnerable spot beneath her ear. "I can't see you. Does that help?"

He was teasing her, still smiling. Hannah could feel him against her skin, and there was no way she could turn him away. "Fine. Stay." As if it didn't matter, she shrugged, went into her bedroom and shut the door.

Then she sat on her bed and stared at that shut door, her body and mind at war as to what they wanted from the man on the other side of it.

HOURS LATER Zach came awake to a low cry from the bedroom, followed by a soft thud. He was off the couch and through the door before he came fully conscious, hitting his knees on the floor in front of the thrashing lump by the bed.

"Hannah." She was flailing wildly in the dark, trapped in the blanket, which had fallen with her. "Hold still, I've got you." It took him a moment to free her, but when she did, she surprised him, leaping to her feet.

There was no light, only the faint moon, so he couldn't be certain, but it seemed as though she was standing over him, chest heaving, glaring with fury.

At *him.* "Hannah?"

She shoved back her hair, her breathing ragged, and he reached out and flipped on the light.

He immediately wished he hadn't. She'd obviously had a nightmare. Her shirt was soaked through, plastered against her skin, which was shiny and lustrous. Her thighs, the ones he'd just been dreaming about having wrapped around him, quivered, and she hugged herself, all while shooting him with those mental daggers.

"*You,*" she said.

"Yes, me." He was still on his knees, unable to take his eyes off the incredible sight she made standing over him. Her full breasts were thrust up by her crossed arms. And from his low vantage point, he could see just a peek-a-boo hint of white panties beneath the hem of her shirt. "A bad dream?"

"Not a bad one, no." Again, she shoved the hair out of her eyes, then dragged in a deep breath. She continued to glare at him as she moved past him, affording him a fantastic view of her perfect rear end.

Then the bathroom door slammed behind her, making him blink. "Hannah?"

"You sleep naked," came her accusing voice.

*Yes.* He hadn't thought about that when he'd raced into the bedroom thinking something was seriously wrong.

"I'm taking a shower," she called out grumpily. "A cold one."

Ah. He got it now, and pleased, he let out a low laugh. "You had a sexual dream. About me."

"Don't let it go to your head," he heard her mutter, then the shower blasted on.

He stared at the closed door. Oh, he'd let it go to his head all right.

She still wanted him.

Denying them both because of an elusive future they couldn't control seemed so wasteful. Surging to his feet, he moved toward the bathroom and knocked softly.

No answer.

Not a "go away," but not exactly an invitation either. His fingers played with the handle, which turned easily in his hand.

She hadn't locked the door.

He stared down at it, and finally decided that he'd take *that* as his invitation.

HANNAH LIED. The water was hot, hot, hot and she stood there beneath the spray of the shower, trying to blank out her mind.

It wasn't working.

All she could think about was Zach; how he made her laugh, how he made her feel alive, vibrant. Sexy.

As she soaped up, the water pounded over her icy skin, chasing away the shivers and warming her until she felt languid, almost lazy. As she soaped, her hands running over the body she washed every single day, she felt...different.

Sexy. Damn that man anyway, because now all she could think about was making love with him.

And making love with Zach was incredible. He was wild and hot, and yes, outrageously sensual. But far more important, somehow in spite of all the sizzle and heat, they'd managed to connect on a deeper level.

Heart and soul.

Sighing, she cranked up the hot water all the more and closed her eyes.

*Heart and soul.*

Wasn't that just the problem?

She heard the bathroom door open one nanosecond before the shower curtain slid aside.

"That's not a cold shower," Zach said.

She shrieked and went to cover herself, but before she could do that, he stepped into the shower, crowding her with his body, his piercing eyes, his voice when he leaned over her, pinning his arms on the tile on either side of her.

"Tell me to leave," he said. "And I will, right now. But look me in the eyes when you tell me, so I believe you, because what *I* believe is that we belong here, together, for as long as we can make this work."

It wasn't easy to think past the fact that he was completely naked, as was she, and now all those rough and ready muscles were hard and glistening, his skin sleek and smooth and hotter than the water that cascaded over his shoulders and back. "You believe...what?"

"I want you," he clarified, looking fierce and primitive, his eyes narrow and glittering. "And you want me."

"No, the other," she managed, forcing herself to look into his eyes. "The part about belonging together."

"You heard me." Now he nudged closer, big and strong and undeniably male. She couldn't look away from him, both enthralled and even a little frightened. How had this happened, how had her feelings for him become so...huge?

He must have seen some of her fear. "Don't ever be afraid of me," he whispered, brushing her dripping hair out of her eyes. His hands were gentle as he stroked them down her body. "I won't hurt you this time."

He was referring to her lost virginity, but that had hardly hurt, and even then, only for a flash. No, what she was afraid of was what he made her *feel*. "You didn't hurt me."

His eyes glittered. "No?"

"No," she whispered.

The heat of the water had a swirl of steam surrounding them, and Hannah felt her senses take over, as if it was all a dream. A dream making her body quiver, a dream making her arch toward him in acquiescence.

Zach bent to kiss her, slow and deep. Without hesitation, she opened her mouth, kissing him back with everything she had, and he groaned. His grip on her tightened, and the kiss went wild with urgency. She felt his callused palms sliding up her thighs, felt him shudder as his hand moved over her bare buttocks, his fingers caressing her.

With every movement, he taught her more about pleasure, more about herself than she could have imagined, and she moved against him, lost in the sensual haze. Then she felt herself lifted, pressed back against the tile wall, held in place by Zach's body.

He lifted his head, his expression dark and passionate. "This isn't for curiosity's sake, or because you're tired of not knowing what pleasure is like," he grated out. "This isn't to get out of *toilet* duty, or to satisfy some bet. This is because I can't stop thinking about you, about your laugh, your voice, your everything, and I want it to be the same for you."

So intense, so sure. It should have terrified her

all the more. Instead, it soothed her. "It's the same for me," she whispered.

He looked at her for a long moment, while her heart jerked painfully in her chest. Then, finally, he bent and kissed her, then bent further and drew a nipple into his mouth, causing her to gasp and arch as heat spread through her. He shifted, covering her other breast with his rough palm. And when his fingers trailed down over her quivering belly, she could hardly stand it because she remembered how he'd made her feel last time, as if she was flying off a cliff without a net.

Suddenly she was in a hurry to feel that way again, because she knew he would catch her, he'd always catch her. His fingers slid lower, lower still, and touched her, evoking a small, helpless sound.

"Do you like that?"

Hard to believe she could get this far with him and suddenly be torn between ecstasy and embarrassment.

"Hannah?" He stopped the magic with his fingers and a whimper escaped her lips before she could stop it.

"Yes," she managed. "But..."

"But?"

"It was dark last time."

"You've seen me before, several times now."

"But...you haven't seen me."

"I want to," he murmured. "I want to see everything—the way your body flushes, the way your nipples go all tight and pouty, the way you pant for air and look at me with that glazed, helpless expression. You drive me wild, Hannah, and I want to see all of it. All of you."

He was touching her again, light, feathery touches over swollen and wet ultrasensitive flesh. Unable to stop herself, she writhed against his hand, and when he pressed open her legs, so that they wrapped around his hips, her head began to swim. She dug her fingers into the muscles of his arms and clung to his hard, warm, welcoming body, unable to believe how close to that edge of the cliff she already was. "Zach..."

"I know. I know— Ahh." He sank a finger into her, making her cry out, and mindless now, she rocked her hips, frantic need slamming into her in relentless waves.

He entered her then, slowly, inch by inch, letting her body accommodate his, letting the heat and pleasure and desperate need intensify. He deepened the kiss as he thrust, pushing deep within her, burying himself to the hilt. "Oh baby," he whispered, and thrust again.

It was so powerful, so raw and...*perfect*. There was tension and unbearable excitement clouding her thoughts, but even through them Hannah knew, this was different, what they had couldn't be found with anyone else.

The water cooled slightly, but it didn't matter, they had more than enough heat between them, and sliding her fingers into his silky hair, she cradled him with her arms and legs, pouring everything she had into the moment, knowing she'd never really lived before now.

The shower thundered over them, their hearts roared as one. Low moans mixed with soft cries. Slick skin against slick skin. Her hips undulated against his as she strained with him toward completion, consumed by the fever of it all.

She felt him shudder and groan, and felt a surge of power at making this strong man so weak with the wanting.

"Come for me now," he urged, gripping her hips, lifting her for a more perfect fit. "Hannah, now...I can't hold back—"

It didn't matter.

Her senses and body exploded in the sweetest, wildest pleasure imaginable, and she cried out.

On and on it went, unending, and she thought

she might even fall, but Zach somehow managed to hold on to her even as his own cry matched hers, his body convulsing as he met his own climax.

# 12

HANNAH CAME AWAKE because her feet were cold. Frozen, as a matter of fact. So was her bare, naked bottom.

It took another moment of muddled confusion to realize this was because she was face-down, sprawled sideways across her bed, with no covers.

She reached down, groping for them, and came in contact with more icy skin, not her own this time. Resorting to opening her eyes, she saw that she had her hand on Zach's equally bare, and equally icy, rear end.

But it was a very fine rear end, as were his long, powerful legs and tight, sleek back.

All gloriously naked.

He too was sprawled sideways over the bed, which as she remembered now, is where they'd collapsed, exhausted, after a most incredible night.

His eyes were still closed, and she noted with

some amusement that he had a slight smile on his face.

Something deep within her reacted at just the sight of him, and it wasn't anything she'd ever experienced before.

Oh, boy.

She was most definitely falling for him. Seriously falling.

One of his eyes opened, and when he saw her, his smile widened as his arm snaked out and grabbed her close.

"We're cold," she said inanely, gasping as he rolled and brought her in contact with his very warm chest and lower body.

"Well, give me a minute, I can change that." His big hands stroked her chilled skin. "Remember how I warmed you last night?"

Yes, she remembered. And blushed furiously with the memory, thank you very much.

"Ah, you do." He gave her a wicked smile.

She'd never forget. He'd warmed her over every single inch of her body until she'd been begging him for more. *Begging*. She wasn't likely to forget how quickly he'd obliged her.

Or how she'd returned the favor, thrilling to the dark, needy sounds she'd dragged out of him.

"Hannah."

She realized his smile had faded and he was watching her with utmost seriousness. In direct contrast, he tenderly stroked her face. "Last night, in the shower...I didn't use a condom."

"Oh." *Oh.*

"I didn't protect you. I've never forgotten before, *never*, and—"

"It...it wasn't all your fault, I forgot too."

His face twisted, and he dropped his forehead to hers. "I'm sorry."

She knew the dangers of unprotected sex, and yet last night she'd never once thought about it. How could that have happened?

"I hate to leave without knowing," he said slowly. "If you're pregnant."

She hated the way her heart constricted at the thought of him going, much more than worrying about the possible consequences of last night.

"I want you to promise to contact me if you are."

"Zach—"

"Promise," he urged, his eyes a fathomless blue. "If you don't, I'm going to stay until I find out for myself."

She stared at him for a long moment, seeing the genuine concern. He *would* stay, she knew that, he would think it his duty.

And in that moment, she couldn't help but wonder, what would it be like to allow herself to be loved by such a man, with this all-consuming passion?

Would she want his baby?

Would she be wishing right now that they'd started a child last night?

"Hannah."

"All right," she murmured. "I promise."

"I mean it. I don't want you to face that alone."

"I promised, Zach. I meant it."

That seemed to relieve him, but all it did was up her confusion factor.

She'd resigned herself to him leaving, or at least had told herself she had, to accepting whatever it was they could share until that time. But if she wasn't careful, she'd be yearning for things like a white lacy wedding dress, a dreamy honeymoon and a house with a white picket fence.

Zach lifted his head to speak, to probably say something that would make her heart squeeze all the more, and she couldn't allow it. So she used the first distraction that came to mind, and tugged his head down to hers, kissed him, deepening it until he moaned and pulled her beneath him.

Talking was forgotten.

TARA AND ALEXI MET in the kitchen early that morning. It wasn't a scheduled business meeting, but a secretive one, which explained why Hannah wasn't invited.

They needed to discuss her.

"She's falling for him," Tara said confidently.

"And he's falling for her, too," Alexi said, but she paced the kitchen. "Still, he's leaving soon and I don't see her just walking away from here to be with him. Not that I want her to go—"

"Of course not! But there can be compromises."

"Well, you would *think* so," Alexi said with a sigh. "But they're both so set in their lives."

"So what are we going to do?"

"Well damn, I don't know. Who would have thought matchmaking would be so darned difficult? We gave her a push with that silly toilet challenge thing, I would have thought she could take it from there." Irritably, Alexi started chewing on her nails. "I swear, you'd think I was the *older* sibling, the way I have to take charge of Zach's life."

"Excuse me?" Zach stepped into the kitchen, brow raised in query. "Take charge of my life? Since when?"

Tara stood. "Well, I'd love to stay but I

have...stuff to do. Yeah, *stuff*." She shot Alexi a long look, smiled weakly at Zach, and left.

"Chicken," Alexi muttered. She forced a bright smile at Zach. "Hey, good morning. How about breakfast?"

"Hold on. I see that look in your eyes, and I know it all too well. You're up to something, and unfortunately for me, it apparently involves my life. So spill it."

"Are you kidding? And risk life and limb?"

"I've never hurt you."

"What about the time you whacked me with a baseball?"

"I was nine and you'd just happened to wobble out on the back porch just as I hit it. I didn't mean to!"

"Uh-huh." She crossed her arms. "And how about the time you nearly lost me at Disneyland?"

"Hey, it's absolutely not my fault you fell asleep behind a rock on Tom Sawyer's island. I searched everywhere!"

Alexi smiled. "That was fun—you should have seen the look on your face when I popped up. You cried."

"I did not!"

"It's okay for a man to cry, Zach. In fact, it makes them sexy."

"I was twelve! And you're still doing it, you're *still* driving me crazy."

"That's why you love me so much."

"Yeah." And because he was in a good mood, and also because he knew she hated it, he ruffled her hair.

She growled and made him laugh. "Love you, too," he said with a grin.

"Oh, Zach." With a sudden fierceness, she grabbed him close in a hug. "And you're leaving again. I'll miss you so much. Why can't you be tired of the big city life by now? Avila really is a terrific place. You could be happy here if you tried."

Slowly, gently, he untangled himself and helped himself to a glass of iced tea, which he downed in two swallows because suddenly his mouth was dry.

And his heart heavy.

In a matter of days he'd be back in Los Angeles, on a new case.

Back to the grind.

Only he didn't think he was ready. For one thing, he was still tired. And for another…

Oh, who the hell was he kidding?

He was no longer tired.

He no longer hurt.

He was even in decent shape. There was no reason why he couldn't go back to work—except that he didn't want to.

He didn't want to leave Hannah.

A longer leave might temporarily solve the problem, but as Hannah had pointed out, that would only make it worse when *he* did go back.

Way worse.

He turned away from his sister's questing, worried gaze and looked out the window, which happened to overlook Hannah's beautiful gardens.

She was out there on her knees, bent over a small pot of daisies. Probably talking to them, he thought with a reluctant smile. She was beautiful out there, with the wind in her hair, the ocean at her back.

And from deep within him came an unrelenting yearning for…for what? And wasn't that just the problem? He couldn't put a name to this terrible aching need, and because he couldn't, he had no idea how to solve it.

"She's very special."

Zach turned his head to look at Alexi, who was

standing solemnly beside him, looking out the same window at the same woman.

"I can see how you look at her," Alexi said. "And the funny thing is, I just *knew* it would be this way between the two of you."

"I belong in Los Angeles, Alexi. And Hannah..." He looked out the window again, saw the slight smile carving her lips as she tended to her beloved plants. "She belongs here."

"No, she belongs with her heart. Which will be with you wherever you are."

"What the hell does that mean?"

"Love," Alexi said simply. "I'm talking about love."

"Alexi—"

"Okay." She sighed. "Fine. We'll do this your way and pretend nothing is happening. Tell me you haven't felt an attraction for her. Tell me you haven't kissed her, not even once, not even to lick off strawberry pie from her shoulder."

"You've been spying on us!"

Alexi merely smiled smugly. "Well, really, Zach. How else do you expect me to help you?"

Zach groaned and turned back to the window.

Hannah was gone.

"Tell me," his sister pressed. "Tell me there's nothing between you two."

"Alexi—"

"Ah-ha! So you *have* been sleeping together!"

"I absolutely did not say that."

"Damn, you know what that means, don't you? Lots of toilet cleaning in my future." But she looked immensely pleased about it. "So...when do you move her down to Los Angeles? I'll miss her, of course, but—"

"She's not moving," Zach said flatly.

"Why?"

"Because I work undercover, for one. I couldn't see her anyway."

"Ever thought about not working undercover?"

All the time, lately. "Yes, actually. But she'd hate it there."

"Oh, right. Too much action and excitement, right?"

"It's not her style. I would never ask her to leave here. Her whole life is here."

"How do you know that for certain until you ask her?"

"I just know, all right?"

Alexi studied him for a long moment, her gaze full of disappointment and a growing anger. "You slept with her."

"Would you stop saying that! This is between me and her!"

"You slept with her," she repeated, undeterred. "You gave her that sparkle in her eyes, the one I've never seen before. You made her happy, dammit. And you're going to leave without looking back?"

"I thought your concern was for *me.*"

"You *are,*" she breathed. "You're going to turn what you had with her into…into a one-night stand! How could you!"

"You're the one who told me to do it!"

"I thought it would mean too much to you to leave if you did. Hannah is *not* the one-night-stand type! You'll kill her!"

"It's *not* a one-night thing," he retorted, nearly as loudly as his sister, who was shouting at him now. "Believe me, we both—"

"We both what, Zach?"

*Hannah.*

She was standing in the doorway of the kitchen with an absolutely indescribable, unreadable look on her face.

"You guys look a little surprised," she noted coolly. "Let me give you a hint." She leaned close and spoke in a stage whisper. "Next time you're talking about someone, you might want to keep your voices down."

Her glorious green eyes were all but shooting daggers at Zach, her cheeks red with anger.

Had he really thought her expression unreadable?

It wasn't any longer, there could be no mistaking that vivid temper.

"And how *dare* you talk about me behind my back. Discussing me as if I don't have a brain in my own head!"

"Hannah—"

"Oh, be quiet, Alexi," Hannah said, not entirely unkindly. But when she turned to Zach, he was quite certain she wouldn't be nearly so gentle with him. "Zach was right," she said staring right at him. "This is between him and me."

"Look, Hannah—"

"Save it," she said succinctly. "For your curiosity's sake, and probably Tara's, yes, Zach and I had a one-night stand. Well, technically, it took more than one night, didn't it, Zach? But who's counting? This may come as a shock to you, Alexi, but I can make my own decisions."

"Oh honey, that's not what I meant—"

Hannah lifted up a hand. "I know. I know you love me, and I also know that you set up that toilet challenge in the hopes of something exactly like this happening. It was a crafty, underhanded, *terrible* thing to do, but I know that in your meddling, nosy way, you thought you were doing the right thing."

Alexi blinked. "Um...yes."

"But it's over, even you must see that. Zach is going home. And I'm—"

She looked away, but not before emotion blazing from her eyes tore him to shreds. "And I'm going to be fine," she whispered. "My life is going to be fine."

He didn't believe that, or didn't want to believe it. If they'd been alone, he might have forced her to look directly into his eyes and say it, but they had a captive audience.

His overly curious, well-meaning, meddling sister.

He glared at her, but Alexi didn't budge. Instead she glared right back and silently refused to give them the privacy he so desperately needed.

With exasperation, he turned to Hannah. "So what now?"

"You leave."

"And?"

"And nothing."

"You want me to stop caring about you? Just turn it off?"

"Try. And you, too," she said to Alexi. "I want this whole thing just dropped, okay? No more tricks, no more matchmaking."

"Ever?" Alexi asked. "Or—"

*"Ever."*

"You going to just ignore me for the rest of my stay?" Zach asked, and was only marginally relieved to see that give her some pause.

"I don't know. You're hard to ignore."

He was quite certain she didn't mean that as a compliment, but he was going to take it as such.

He had no choice, it was all he had.

# 13

ZACH FOLLOWED HER. Hannah knew this by the way the back of her neck tingled in delicious anticipation.

Clearly her body had not gotten the message her brain had sent it.

*Stop lusting after him.*

She'd have to work on it.

Well, she had the rest of her life to do that, or at least the next ten years until he decided to show up again.

Instead of acknowledging him, as a grown-up, *mature* sort of woman would have done, she kept walking. In fact, she sped up her pace, toeing off her sandals and scooping them up in her fingers so that her toes curled in the sand with each step she took.

He was probably following her just to make sure she wasn't falling apart after that ridiculous little snit of hers in the kitchen.

God, she wished she hadn't done that, hadn't entered the kitchen as if she was a queen bee, telling two of the most important people in her life that she wanted them to stop caring about her.

How stupid.

How juvenile.

She *liked* that they cared about her. Actually, she liked it too much, she depended on it.

And as for Zach and what they'd shared...she liked that, too.

She just didn't like that she'd fallen for him, when falling for him hadn't been a smart thing to do. Oh sure, they would have phone calls in their future. E-mail, faxes, etc. Maybe even the occasional stolen weekend.

Maybe.

But Zach was a cop, which statistically speaking, meant he was married to his job. She had his last case as hard evidence, when he'd gone undercover and hadn't surfaced for one year, and only then because he'd been shot.

"Definitely not dealing with this well," she muttered, startled to realize it was nearly dark and that she'd come a mile down the beach, to the secluded little bay Tara jokingly referred to as Make-Out Rock.

By the time she walked to the far side, near the bluffs, the sun had disappeared completely, leaving an incredibly dark, gorgeous night sky.

She felt it again, that little shiver of awareness that told her Zach was near. She turned, finding him only ten feet away; tall, dark, gorgeous and silent.

Any light she might have used to determine his mood was gone. He was silhouetted by an early moon, his face in the shadows. All she could see was his concerned gaze, which stoked the tornado of feelings just beneath her surface.

"As you can see," she said calmly. "I'm not swimming in a storm. I'm not in danger of drowning. I'm perfectly safe."

"Yes."

Oh fine, *he* was going to be the reasonable one. "And actually, if I wanted to swim right now, I would. And you know what else? After you're gone, I might even..."

"What, Hannah?"

*Never be the same.*

She was never going to be the same.

Her throat burned with the tears she refused to shed because she didn't dare give in to them or she'd never stop.

There was no one around, no lights, nothing but the moon and the stars. The two of them were in their own little world, protected from view by the bluffs. A breeze danced over them, making

Hannah's skin turn to gooseflesh, and while she stared at the bumps covering her arms, Zach shrugged out of his denim jacket and held it out.

Somehow, that small, chivalrous gesture, the one that meant he hadn't listened to her when she demanded he stop caring about her, broke her control. "Once again, I'm taking something from you," she said. "Let's see...first it was your body, and now—"

"It's just a damn jacket." He placed it around her shoulders.

"I'm fine," she said in a much smaller voice now. "Really I am. I don't need you, I just somehow...think I do."

"Is needing me so bad?"

"It is when I have no idea *how* you feel."

"I need you more than I need my next breath."

"You...do?"

"Yeah." He zipped up the jacket, his fingers lingering at her neck, then her jaw. Slowly he cupped her face, tipped it up and smiled. "I know how fiercely independent you are. I even know why, but that isn't what this is about."

"What is it about?"

"You. And me. Enjoying each other, wanting to be together. Sharing, laughing, talking, touching. We're drawn to each other, helplessly drawn, you can't fight it."

"Guess I haven't had much experience at this."

"Neither have I," he admitted, and at her startled look, he let out a rueful laugh. "Not with *meaningful* relationships, that is."

"You haven't had time?"

"I haven't *made* time." He hadn't taken his hands off her, and now he ran them down her arms to her hands, linking them together with his. "I've never wanted to until now."

Somehow that admission touched her unbearably, because she thought maybe he was saying if things were only different, he would have wanted a meaningful relationship with *her*.

She liked knowing that.

In fact, once he was gone, it would be all she had.

"Maybe making time is something I haven't done either," she said, wanting to be honest. "I always thought it was because I was too busy, but I think maybe I did that on purpose. Used the demands on my time as an excuse not to let anyone close."

"Life can get awfully lonely that way."

"I kept myself busy, so busy I never really noticed. I had Alexi and Tara. And the lodge."

"So what changed?"

"You. It was you. Everything changed that night you came back. I decided to go for it. To, for once, let someone in. Only it got out of control so fast." She shook her head, her throat tight. "I couldn't stop the feelings, the emotions, and even when I told myself over and over again it was all temporary, I still couldn't stop them."

"Me, either." The moonlight glinted in his hair as he brought one of their joined hands up to his mouth, brushing his lips over her skin, softening her heart all the more. "I'm learning sometimes that's okay. You have to trust yourself."

"I...trust you."

"That's good." He leaned close to stare deep into her eyes. "Because I trust you back."

"But I don't want a long-distance relationship."

A half smile curved his lips as he drew her close against his wonderfully warm body. "Well, at least you're admitting you want one."

Oh yes, she wanted one. She hadn't even realized it, not until he'd come back into her life and shown her what she was missing, but she wanted that with all her heart.

And now she couldn't have it. "Zach..."

As if reading her thoughts, he kissed her; a soft,

soul-searching kiss that touched her very soul. Her body took over, made its wants known. She was already pressed against him; it took little effort to slide her arms around his neck, even less to tip her face up.

"We have right now," he murmured. "We don't have to figure it all out this minute, it can be a problem for tomorrow."

True.

They did still have tomorrow. But didn't they deserve more than just one more day?

"You're cold." He ran his hands down her back. "We need to get back."

"I'm not cold." And she wasn't, those faint shivers he'd felt were something else entirely. "Kiss me." And because she couldn't wait, she tugged his head to hers and claimed his mouth.

"Keep that up," he muttered when they came up for air, "and I'm going to kiss every inch of you. Right here."

To ensure that was exactly what happened, Hannah nipped his jaw, then his ear. With a low groan, Zach roughly took her mouth. Thrusting her fingers into his thick hair, she opened her lips beneath his onslaught and sank into the heat of the passion that never failed to flare between them at the slightest touch.

"Here?" she murmured.

"Here." And he took them both down to the sand.

They were completely alone with the waves, the wind, the night sky. And with Hannah in his arms, Zach found he had everything he wanted.

Her mouth was slow and hot and demanding, making him forget about their uncertain and troubled future. They had now, right now, and he wasn't going to waste one precious second of it.

The pounding of the waves was in sync with the drum of pleasure beating through his veins, to the excitement he knew pounded through Hannah as well. Pressed so tightly to her, he could feel the erratic leap of her heart, could hear the dark, needy sounds she made as he ran his hands over her.

She spread his jacket over the sand, then looked at him as they faced each other on their knees. For a long moment, neither of them moved.

Then his palm covered her breast, possessing her, claiming her, and she arched her back, accepting, seeking more.

His thumb slid over just the very tip of her breast, teasing, but it wasn't enough for him, and if he believed the heat in her gaze, it wasn't enough for her, either. He pulled off her sweater, trailing his fingers lightly over the edges of her bra until he came to the front hook, which easily fell open under his touch.

Her gaze flew up to his, wide and glossy, and when his callused fingers rasped over her bare breasts she moaned and let her head fall back on her shoulders. He slid the silk completely off her, exposing her to the night sky and his own hungry gaze. Her nipples were hard and thrust up, two tight, begging peaks. He bent his head and curled his tongue over first one, then the other, while she quivered and whispered his name over and over again in a hoarse, needy voice. She clung to him, and pulled him down onto the jacket, so that she bore all his weight.

Cupping her face, he looked down at her, certain she was the most beautiful woman he'd ever seen. Her lips were open and swollen from his kisses, her bare skin creamy and lush in the moonlight. Her breasts, still wet from his mouth, glistened enticingly, and his feelings for her nearly overwhelmed him. "Hannah—"

"I know." Her eyes reflected all he felt and mirrored her own feelings back.

He kissed her mouth, her neck, then shifted, moving down to her bare, quivering belly. His hands slid over her thighs, her calves, then back up, beneath her skirt now, bringing the material up as he went, exposing her inch by inch to his hungry gaze. He put his hands on her thighs and opened them, settling himself between so he could see her panties, which were tiny, just another scrap of silk, easily moved aside.

"Zach?"

"Shh," he whispered, soothing her with his hands, running them up and down her legs. "I'm going to keep my promise. Every single inch, Hannah."

"I don't think—"

"No thinking allowed," he murmured huskily, bending to his task. He blew a hot breath at the juncture of her thighs and heard the breath back up in her throat. "I'm going to kiss you until you lose it. I want to watch."

"You—"

His mouth touched her then, and whatever she'd planned to say came out as a sigh of surrender.

She tasted like heaven, and she moved like it, too. Shifting wildly, panting, she went as crazy as he already was. He nibbled and stroked, getting hotter by the second, but it wasn't until he drew her into his mouth and sucked that she arched like a bow, shuddering, shuddering, shuddering as her release rushed through her.

Slowly he softened the touch of his mouth, swirling his tongue over her as she came back to her senses. Lifting his head, holding her gaze, he adjusted her panties and slowly, regretfully, straightened her skirt. Before he could change his mind and take her again without protection—and the consequences be damned—he pulled her up and reached for her bra to close it.

"What—wait," she protested, trembling and damp. "I want you..."

The tension in his body was so tight that he thought his jaw might shatter. "We can't."

Her hands slid over him anyway, cupping him right through his jeans. He was hard and ready. "No protection," he managed through his teeth, trying to take her hands off him, but she wouldn't allow it.

Instead, his stubborn Hannah pressed him down on the jacket where she'd just laid, open and vulnerable and in surrender.

She sent him a wicked smile.

"Hannah." He licked his dry lips and tasted her on them, which only made his condition all the more impossible to bear. "We can't," he said hoarsely.

"Maybe not in the way you think." She slid her hands beneath his T-shirt, over his ribs and nipples, which caused him to jerk.

"Hannah—"

"Good?" she murmured, leaning over him and watching him carefully. Her skin was still flushed, her eyes hot and hungry. And also just a touch nervous, he realized as tenderness and a good amount of possessiveness swamped her.

"Does this feel good?" she asked, her fingertips just barely scraping over his skin, making the muscles in his stomach dance. His erection strained against the buttons of his jeans.

"Good isn't quite the word I'd use," he managed.

"No?" She bit her lower lip as she sat back on her heels, staring at the buttons on his jeans. Then her fingers were there, fumbling a bit as she opened them one by one.

Pop. Pop. Pop.

"What word *would* you use then?" she wondered.

"I'd say—" His words broke off on a helpless moan as she slid her hands into his opened jeans, wrapping her fingers around him to gently squeeze.

"You'd say...what?" Now she used those fingers to give him a long, slow, tortuous stroke. Heat pooled in his loins, surging, burning heat, and he figured he had about five seconds of control left.

Maybe.

Then she kneeled between his legs, just as he had hers only moments before, smiled innocently at him—he was beginning to mistrust that innocent smile—and licked the very tip of him.

He nearly came off the jacket. "Hannah!"

She lifted her head. "Is that *Hannah, yes,* or *Hannah, I really hate that?* Because quite honestly, Zach, I'm making all this up as I go along."

He might have been able to answer her, but that was before she once again bent her head. This time her tongue darted out, licking a scorching path upward, upward, and then she hovered over him, her breath hot and teasing as she hesitated.

Helplessly, he strained toward her. "Please," was torn from his throat, though he had no idea what he was begging for. He hadn't expected her to do this, and with his last bit of energy, he slid his fingers into her hair, meaning to lift her away.

But then she took him into her wet, hot mouth, and he was gone, lost, completely out of himself. She simply continued, wrapping her arms around him as he convulsed with a harsh groan, and as the powerful shudders of completion shook him, she held him all the tighter, showing him with actions what she hadn't been able to do with words.

SOMEHOW THEY MADE IT back to the lodge, and to Hannah's room. Once there, they stumbled into bed, found the box of condoms, and turned to each other again.

Then again.

And finally, near dawn, they slept.

Until the phone rang.

"Sorry," came Alexi's voice in Hannah's ear. "Honey, I'm sorry to call so early, but Zach has a call."

Hannah's brain was slow to respond, and it wasn't just from being tired. Being held by Zach, close to his heart, impeded her thought process as well.

"He's with you?" Alexi asked.

Oh, yeah. His arms were curled protectively about her. He nuzzled sleepily at her ear.

"He's here," she said with a smile.

"It's his captain, Hannah. Thought I should warn you."

His captain. His work. Oh God. "Oh."

"Yeah, *oh.*" Alexi managed to convey her sorrow, her regret and her own anger all in that one word. "Tell him line one."

Hannah handed Zach the phone.

He frowned down at the receiver as if it were a poisonous snake. "For me?"

"It's your work."

His gaze searched hers, deep and unrelentingly intense. But he took the phone.

And in that moment she knew. Her little interlude was over.

Zach was really leaving.

# 14

SHE HAD TO give him credit, Hannah thought, two terminally long days later.

He'd said goodbye.

If their positions had been reversed, she might have been tempted to escape those last painful few moments.

And they had been painful.

But she'd watched Zach pack, his eyes solemn and sorrowful. She'd listened to him explain that there was some big raid planned for the next night and that the department was short-handed, that they wouldn't have called him back two days early unless they desperately needed him.

Hannah had watched him drive away, pretending her heart hadn't all but stopped in her chest, pretending she didn't love him.

Oh yeah, she loved him. With everything she had, and yet she hadn't told him. Maybe he loved her back, but because she hadn't been brave enough to share her feelings, she might never know.

He'd called each day, and each day she'd managed to miss that call, maybe on purpose. Hearing his voice would have broken through her almost pleasant numbness.

On the third day, a pot of daisies arrived.

*"Talk to them for me,"* the note said. *"Love, Zach."*

Love.

Just like that, the blessed numbness deserted her.

She managed to make it to her room before completely falling apart. And since she'd been holding on to it so long, it took forever to let it all out.

How did one fall in love so fast? More to the point, *how was she supposed to get over it?*

A gentle knock sounded at her door, but she ignored it. After her self-pity jag she didn't have the energy to talk.

The knock came again, firmer this time, and then both Tara and Alexi crowded into the room.

"That was locked," she muttered.

"Love conquers all." Tara plopped to the bed. "Even locked doors."

Alexi held up a set of keys and jingled them before sitting down on the bed as well. "These helped. Oh Hannah, don't shut us out." Tears filled her eyes. "We miss him, too."

Which started a mutual tissue-fest, but finally, with a sniff, Hannah knew what she had to do.

Maybe she'd known all along. "I love you guys," she said softly. "You're my two best friends in the entire world, and you're my family."

"But you're leaving." Tara squeezed her hands as a new set of tears filled her eyes. "Aren't you?"

"I have to," Hannah whispered. She looked at Alexi, feeling a little nervous, but oddly calm at the same time. "I love him. I have to tell him."

"He loves you, too."

"I don't know that for sure." But she never would unless she did this. "But if he does, and if he wants me to, I'm going to stay there. I have to."

"We've never been separated, not in all these years," Alexi said shakily, hugging Hannah hard. "But I do understand, because I love him, too. Go be happy. We'll be here for you."

"Take your time," Tara added. "We've got the

toilets covered. We'll deal with the business stuff however we need to."

Hannah's heart was racing now that she'd made the decision. "So...how do I tell him?"

Alexi laughed. "That's the easy part! Go find him and...and just blurt it out."

*Just tell him.* Why hadn't she already done it? Why hadn't *he?*

He wouldn't, she thought she understood that now. He would never ask her to give up a part of herself for him. "It was much easier when I was only trying to seduce him."

"Well, you could start with that," Alexi suggested. "Wrap yourself up in red ribbon and have yourself delivered to his doorstep."

"Or sneak into his bed and wait there," Tara said.

"Or pop out of a cake at his station."

Hannah had to laugh. "I think I'll come up with something on my own. But thanks."

ZACH LASTED approximately one day. The bust went down without a hitch.

But then, as he knew he would, he got a new assignment, even deeper undercover than the last time, and something inside him said no.

He just couldn't do it.

Instead he researched getting a transfer; anywhere near or in Avila. The jobs available were sorely limited, but with his connections and referrals, he discovered an opening for deputy sheriff.

No undercover, no days at a time being gone from home.

Sounded perfect.

So did the change of pace. Yes, there'd been a time when he'd needed all that adventure and risk, but his needs had changed.

Avila's slower pace would allow him a personal life. A love life. A family life. He couldn't wait. He leased his condo to a new officer. Giving up his place was a risky move, but he knew his heart.

He should have known it sooner. His only excuse was that he'd been living on automatic, just working, working, working, not realizing it until he'd been shot and unable to do his job.

He'd called Norfolk Inn several times, missing Hannah each time, which was really just as well. He hadn't wanted to do this over the phone. He'd needed to see her face when he told her what he'd done.

When he told her that he loved her.

It was possible he was more scared now than he'd ever been in his life, and he'd been in plenty of terrifying positions before.

But only three days after he'd left Avila, he drove back up the coast to face his future.

HANNAH STARED at the young man who'd opened the condo door. She was startled because...well, because he wasn't Zach.

Plus he'd just given her a shocking announcement.

"What do you mean he doesn't live here anymore?" She couldn't have heard right. She had Zach's address in her hand, written in Alexi's own handwriting.

The man lifted a shoulder, looking apologetic. "He left this morning. He's gone."

Gone.

Okay, maybe he meant gone as in grocery shopping, not gone as in *gone*. "Do you know where he went?"

"Well..." The young man wrinkled his forehead as he strained to remember. "He said he was going back to paradise."

"Paradise? But he lives here in L.A."

"Not anymore, he leased the place to me."

"Oh, I see," she said, but she didn't.

He seemed to take pity on her confusion. "Norfolk Inn? Yes, that's it. Norfolk Inn. He said the place was home."

Blood roared in her head now, so that she practically stuttered her thanks.

Only one question remained now—had Zach gone back to Avila because it was home, or had he gone back because of her?

FATE WAS NOT on Hannah's side. The freeways in Los Angeles were at a complete standstill. Then she got a flat tire outside of Santa Barbara and had to call for roadside service.

By the time she exited off Highway 1 and rode into Avila, it was past midnight. Her eyes were gritty with exhaustion and a tension that no amount of quickly downed junk food had eased.

The porch light of the lodge was welcoming, as was the ocean breeze and the unique feeling of being home.

There truly was no place like it.

And Zach was inside, or so she hoped.

Nerves leaped like butterflies in her stomach as she quietly let herself in. Silence greeted her. No one was in the kitchen or the living room, or in their downstairs office.

Everyone was asleep. She checked the front register for Zach, knowing it was unlikely he'd be officially checked in, but she was hoping all the same.

He wasn't listed.

And she could hardly go knock on each door, waking up guests, hoping to get it right.

Disappointment was a bitter pill. Completely deflated, not to mention exhausted, she entered her room, shut the door and sagged against the wall.

Where had he gone?

Kicking off her shoes, she headed directly for the bedroom.

*Sleep*, she thought, her throat tight, heart heavy.

But as she stepped toward the bed, it came alive.

Then she was blinking as the lamp was abruptly flipped on, staring in stunned shock at Zach, who stared right back at her.

"Thank God," she heard him mutter before he tossed aside the covers and surged to his feet.

He was totally and gloriously naked.

"What's going on?" he demanded, putting his

hands on his hips and glaring at her. "Where were you?"

"Didn't...didn't Alexi and Tara tell you?" She had a hard time keeping her eyes on his because he was so absolutely beautiful. And so annoyed.

Which, when she thought about it, was how *she* should feel.

"I've been worried sick!" he said. "Alexi and Tara wouldn't tell me a thing. In fact, they took one look at me and started laughing."

"Were you naked at the time?"

He looked down at himself and swore, then yanked up the jeans he'd dropped on the foot of the bed. "No, I wasn't naked. I got naked after figuring out you weren't coming back." He shoved one foot into his jeans, then nearly fell over, swore again and ended up kicking the material away.

"I don't need pants for this," he said, then before she could blink, he had her flat on her back on her own bed, and covered by his very large, very male body.

"Now," he said, deliberately sliding his hands along her arms, which were over her head, until he held her hands in his, effectively holding her captive. "You were about to tell me what's going on."

Good Lord, he was so fierce, so intense, so absolutely sexy she could hardly see straight. Not to mention her heart had just about leaped out of her chest at the mere sight of him.

But now that her big moment was here, and she could tell him how she felt, she found her tongue had tied itself into knots. "Um...why don't *you* start?"

"Okay," he said with such mock compliance, she narrowed her eyes.

Zach was never compliant.

"I love you. And I think you love me," he said conversationally. "I also think that you've been telling yourself you couldn't possibly fall in love—the timing's bad, it happened too fast, whatever. You'd rather pretend it doesn't exist."

"I don't pretend!"

"Really? So you expect me to believe you made love with me that first time because you didn't want to clean toilets?"

"I already told you it was more than that. I knew it right away. It was just..."

"Too big to handle?"

"Yes, and I'd only known you a few days, Zach. *A few days*. It terrified me."

"You've known me all your life. What happened then, what has happened ever since, has nothing to do with anything but us and how we feel for each other."

"Yes," she whispered. And there was more, so much more, but she was feeling a little shy now that the moment was here and Zach was on top of things.

Literally.

Honestly, she was having trouble putting thoughts together in her head with all his intensity and gorgeous eyes, not to mention his bare, hard, warm body stretched out over hers.

"Did I tell you the bust went just like clockwork?" he asked calmly. "That I was given a new undercover assignment? And, oh by the way, I quit my job?"

She went utterly still. "You *what?* You didn't tell me that's what you were going to do."

"I know." He gentled his grip on her, letting go of her hands to cup her face. "I was afraid, Hannah."

"You're not afraid of anything."

"Oh, yes I am. I'm afraid you don't really understand how I feel about you. I'm afraid you don't feel the same way back. I'm afraid of living without you in my life."

When she opened her mouth to speak, he leaned down and softly brushed his lips over hers. "Don't interrupt. I'm trying to make sure I make you feel so loved you can't turn me down."

Turn him down...for what?

But then he was kissing her again. "There," he whispered, smiling down at her, his eyes filled with so many things she could hardly breathe. "That's the expression I was looking for."

"Dazed?"

"No. Love." He stroked her jaw with his thumbs. "Where was I? Oh, yes, so I quit my job."

"But you loved that job!"

"I love being a cop, but what I didn't love was being in Los Angeles, working undercover for so long that I was no longer Zach Thomas, but just a man existing. No family. No friends. No you."

"You didn't know then—"

He kissed her again, a long, deep, deliciously messy kiss this time, and he didn't pull back until they were both unsteady. "No, I didn't know I wanted you in my life, that didn't come until after the shooting, but I figured it out after I saw you again. One look, Hannah, and I knew, even if I didn't want to. It was as if I was looking into a mirror that night, and I saw my soul mate. I just didn't know how to accept it until I faced leaving here. Faced being without you. And even then I kept denying the truth, until I was back in Los Angeles and couldn't deny it anymore."

"So you just quit your job? But I was quitting mine! I went down to Los Angeles to find you and—"

"And I was here." Zach started to laugh, shook his head, then lowered his forehead to hers. "That's why Alexi and Tara got such a kick out of this. And I was clueless."

"You wouldn't have been if you'd told me!"

"Or if *you'd* told *me*." His eyes were alive with hope and joy. "You came after me. Do you have any idea how that makes me feel?"

"Jobless?" she asked, still stunned that he'd given up everything for her. *Everything*. The depth of his love amazed and humbled her. Thrilled her.

"I'm still going to be a cop," he said. "Just here."

"In Avila. You'd...do that?" she whispered. "Really? You would? But..."

"I would and did. Don't you get it yet, Hannah? I want to be with you." Nervousness leaped into his gaze when he said that, making her realize she hadn't been honest enough back with him.

"Do you know why I went to L.A.?" she asked him. "Why I walked away from the lodge and Alexi and Tara?"

"No, but you're going to tell me, because you're not leaving this bed until you do." His body pressed into hers.

"Mmm. I love the feel of you wrapped around me," she whispered, arching into him a little.

His eyes, already hot, went hotter, and he thrust a thigh between her legs, spreading them, making room for himself. "Do you?" He dipped down to scrape his teeth over the spot beneath her ear, making her shiver with delight. "I love the feel of you wrapped around me, too."

All she could do was hum her agreement because he'd shifted that hard thigh and was rubbing it against her legs, pressing down until she spread even farther for him.

At the very intimate contact, they both sighed.

"You were going to tell me something important," he reminded her thickly, once again rocking against the very core of her, which sent shock waves of desire through her body.

"I—" She broke off with a startled gasp when he slid the straps of her sundress down, exposing her breasts to his gaze. She felt her nipples harden into two tight, aching tips.

"You what?" he urged, palming the weight of them in his palms, using his thumbs to rasp back and forth over her nipples so that she could hardly breathe. "Hannah?"

"I—" He swept the skirt of her sundress up to her waist, whisked off her panties and settled back against her, so that they were skin to skin.

"Wait," she gasped. "I wanted to tell you when I could actually see straight…I wanted you to know how much more than just lust this was…I wanted—"

"You're right." Utterly unselfconsciously, given that he was totally naked and clearly aroused, he rose off of her and kneeled on the bed.

"No distractions," he promised, lifting his hands, a small smile playing on his lips, but his eyes were completely serious. "So tell me why you came to L.A., why you would have given up everything you cared about."

Not as completely at ease with her own nudity as he was, Hannah sat, and demurely tugged down the hem of her skirt, which made Zach's lips quirk, but he said nothing, not even when she crossed her arms over her chest, bit her lip and finally looked him in the eyes.

"I would have given up ten times as much," she said. "Actually, I would have given up my entire life to be with you."

"Why, Hannah?"

"Because I love you. I love you with all my heart." She smiled through misty eyes. "I think I always have, and I know I always will." Her whole world seemed perfect. Almost. "I just don't want you to give up anything for me, I mean it." She squeezed him close. "Nothing. If you still want Los Angeles, then—"

"No." He smiled into her hair. "But I don't want you to give up anything for me, either. Except for maybe some time. You work too hard."

"I think I have a good reason to have regular days off now."

"Let me give you a better one." He cupped her face to stare into her eyes. "Marry me."

She went still. "I don't think I'm pregnant. The timing was wrong."

A flicker of disappointment crossed his face but then he smiled. "One thing at a time then. Be with me forever, Hannah."

Her smile widened. "I like forever."

"Good."

"I want your children." Her heart threatened to burst with happiness. "I want a little girl and a little boy."

He stared at her from suspiciously damp eyes. "Is that a yes, then?"

"It's more than a yes." She smiled through her own tears. "It's a promise."

From the other side of the door, Alexi and Tara grinned their delight and hugged for joy.

This Christmas, experience
the love, warmth and magic that
only Harlequin can provide with
Mistletoe
Magic
a charming collection from
BETTY NEELS
MARGARET WAY REBECCA WINTERS
Available November 2000
HARLEQUIN®
Makes any time special™